NEW BEGINNINGS

A THISTLE BAY SHORT STORY

CLAIRE ANDERS

A CIP catalogue record for this book is available from the British Library.

Published by TLC Publications Ltd

Cover Design by MiblArt

ISBN 978-1-8381777-9-9 (ebook)

ISBN 978-1-8381777-8-2 (print)

For Evie & Scout

NEW BEGINNINGS

A Thistle Bay Short Story

When Josef's wife of fifty years unexpectedly passes away, his plans for the future are thrown into disarray. His four grown-up children arrive to help him deal with the practicalities of death and where he goes from here. But it's not long before he's feeling smothered and is longing for an escape.

Eva was the adventurous one in their marriage and Josef is lost without her. As his children plan his future, Josef has a decision to make. Should he accept what he sees as the inevitability of old age or can he find a life after death?

1

———

Josef Fischer had never seen a dead body before. He certainly hadn't expected the first dead body he saw to be his wife's. The lines on Eva's face had melted away, leaving a waxy sheen on her skin, and the smile that had adorned her face every day of their fifty-year marriage was gone.

'She looks at peace, Dad.' Nadja was the eldest of their four children and the only one that still lived in Berlin. He had called an ambulance, knowing it was already too late, then he had called his daughter.

Josef nodded for Nadja's benefit. Eva didn't look at peace. She didn't look in pain, or even unhappy. She just didn't look like herself. The image of her now – her tiny frame lying motionless in their bed – was one he hoped would fade from his mind quickly.

They'd spoken about death. That happens when you're in your seventies, he supposed. Josef had been of the opinion that when you were dead, you were dead. That was it. Eva had thought otherwise. She was convinced your soul went someplace else. Now, as he stared at her empty face, there was no feeling of finality. His wife's essence was most definitely gone; it had slipped away from the body that had held it safely for seventy-one years. But he could see that it just wasn't possible for that essence to evaporate into nothingness.

He smiled. That woman had always been right.

They had planned every detail of their funerals, not that Josef had much to plan – he wanted a simple affair that would cost the children as little as possible. Eva, ever-practical, had created a separate bank account that held enough money to pay for both their funerals and she'd given Nadja access to the account so the children didn't have to cover the costs themselves upfront. A folder in their filing cabinet contained lists of her specific plans. She had thought of everything.

It wasn't that Eva wanted an expensive funeral, although they both knew that even basic ones were expensive. She just had very particular wishes about what she would like to be included in her service and she had said that Josef would forget.

He would have.

All these were details he'd never thought he would need. Women were supposed to live longer than men. Eva should have been burying him.

Josef studied his wife now and the only detail he could remember for the ceremony was that she wanted 'Somewhere Over the Rainbow' to be played – with the English lyrics – at the end. It was their song. Or, at least, it had become their song. Even the children loved it. Diane, their youngest child, had once asked her mother to sing the song in German. Eva had refused. She'd said the song was so beautiful it could only be sung the way the writers had intended it to be. She didn't have the same loyalty to the original melody, however, and had adopted a more upbeat version of the tune over the years.

Josef's mother used to sing it in English too. She was French and his father was German, but his parents had spent the last years of the Second World War together on the east coast of Scotland. Josef had been born there and the family had only moved to Germany when Josef was ten years old. He'd met Eva five years later: his mother had been singing in the garden and her mellow voice, together with the English words, had drawn Eva out from the apartment upstairs. Josef and Eva were fifteen-year-old neighbours who became best friends first, then sweethearts, then husband and wife.

Now, he was a widower. Alone for the first time in decades.

Josef stood up and his hand instinctively reached out for Eva's. Hovering over her pale flesh, he shook his head. His wife's touch was always warm. Even in the depths of winter her hands could soften butter in seconds, which was useful for his toast in the morning; not so useful when he was making flaky pastry. Warm – that's how he wanted to remember her.

He trudged to the living room weighed down by the unfairness of life and stood before the window of their ground-floor lounge. He squinted in the spring sunshine at the wall across the street that was pockmarked with bullet holes. Many a visitor had asked Josef if the daily reminder of such a horrific time in human history bothered him. It didn't. Reminders had been left everywhere across the city, but he understood why. When the world forgets is when the world risks making the same mistakes again Eva had allowed her fingers to circle the jagged edges of those holes whenever she passed by them and she would smile, grateful

for the opportunities their four children had as a conse-
quence of the strength and sacrifice of so many.

'She died peacefully in her sleep,' he heard Nadja say.
She was on the telephone to someone – he wasn't sure who.
'Yes, it's the best way to go, isn't it?'

Is it? Perhaps. But not when you're only seventy-one
years old with dreams yet to be realised.

Josef turned away from the window and dropped into
his favourite chair. His forearms gravitated to the well-worn
armrests of the deep-red fabric chair. They'd talked about
selling the house and moving somewhere else, especially
this last year. Eva had dreamed of a garden and a little house
on the coast. She was the more adventurous one in their
relationship and she loved travelling. Whereas Josef had
been reluctant to leave his bakery for more than a week
once or twice a year, Eva had taken six holidays in the last
nine months.

Retirement wasn't something Eva had ever pressured
Josef to consider. She'd known he had to get there in his
own time. But she had become more demanding of his time
in the last two years – something he was thankful for now.
He had reduced his hours at the bakery so they could spend
evenings out enjoying dinner and time with friends. He'd
even taken a month off completely to enjoy a whole week
with each of their children and grandchildren. Those were
experiences he never would have had without Eva's quiet
demands and it was those experiences that had prompted
his decision to sell the bakery.

Stefan, who had worked with Josef for twenty-five years,
was always open about his desire to buy the bakery when
Josef was ready to sell up – as soon as he learned that none
of the Fischer children were bakers, or interested in
becoming bakers, he let it be known that he would be inter-

ested in taking over. Josef suspected poor Stefan hadn't expected to have to wait so long, but he was loyal. And patient. An occupational requirement.

The phone clicked back into its cradle and Nadja slumped down into the chair opposite Josef.

'How are you?' he asked her.

Nadja nodded. 'That was Mrs Gedeck from next door, checking in to see how you are. How on earth she knew is beyond me.'

'Perhaps she caught the doctor leaving. Or she saw you arriving early, without the children, and guessed something was up. Her chair is positioned right in the window. She listens to the radio and spends all day watching everyone coming and going.'

Nadja swallowed. 'She thought it was you,' she said, her voice barely perceptible.

Josef watched his daughter – her blonde hair that disguised the odd silver strand, her pale skin, the abundance of water in her eyes and the pain etched on her face. She was the only one to inherit Eva's complexion; the other three had his darker colouring. 'It should have been me.'

'Dad, don't say that. It shouldn't have been either of you. You're too young for this.' The words caught in her throat. 'She was so healthy,' she whispered.

The thudding on his front door brought Josef to his feet and he heard Nadja blow her nose behind him. Josef opened the door and made to greet the woman on the other side. She murmured into her mobile phone and raised a finger, indicating for him to wait his turn, as if he had been the one to knock on her door.

'Hello,' she said when she had finished her call, dropping her phone into the pocket of her long black coat. 'I'm

Ada Huber, the undertaker. I spoke with you on the phone earlier.'

'With my daughter Nadja.'

'Indeed.' Not waiting to be invited, she glided past him and into the living room. She was dressed head to toe in black and carried a laptop and a canary-yellow cardboard file that jarred the senses. The colour seemed inappropriate. Surely a more sombre colour would be better suited to this kind of situation.

Josef followed her and sat down, thanking Nadja for the tray of coffee and cherry cake she had sliced and brought through. He stared at the thick end slice of cake – at its rough edges and crust-like appearance. There was only one. Eva had sliced the other end off the evening before and had eaten it with a dollop of cold custard. And now she was gone.

Ada took a seat on the sofa opposite him. The inappropriate file was placed by her feet and she opened the laptop, now resting on her knees. 'I'm sorry for your loss,' she said, inclining her head like a robot.

Josef sat motionless. He couldn't decide if this was the first death she had attended or if she had become so numbed over the years that she couldn't appreciate how bad a first impression she was making.

Nadja cleared her throat and offered Ada coffee.

'Thank you,' she said. 'Coffee would be good.'

As Nadja poured, Ada thumped away at the keys on her laptop, oblivious to the irritation simmering deep within Josef.

A mobile phone blared out with an offensive ringtone that reverberated around the room. Nadja jumped at the piercing sound as Ada fished the phone out of her pocket, glanced at the screen and sighed.

'I'm with a customer right now,' she said, answering. 'I'll call you back when I'm done here.'

A customer. Josef served customers in his bakery. He was a customer when he purchased his coffee at the café on the corner, and when he had bought the cherries that now peeked out from the sliced cake on the table in front of him that his beloved Eva had complimented only last night. The transactional nature of the word was as aggravating as her canary-coloured file. He waited for her to end her latest call then stood up.

'Miss Huber, I'm afraid this isn't going to work out.'

Confusion spread across her forehead. 'I'm not sure I understand.'

'Given the disregard with which you treat the living, I have no intention of allowing you near my wife.'

'*Dad!*'

'I'll leave you to show her out, if you don't mind, Nadja.'

Ada looked as astonished as his daughter, but he hoped she would reflect on their encounter in time and handle her next *customer* with more sensitivity.

Josef took a deep breath, scooped up a mug of coffee and gulped it down.

As well as the cherry cake, Josef had baked a rye bread the day before, which Nadja had used to make sandwiches for lunch. They sat uneaten in the centre of the kitchen table; the fragrant dill pickles did nothing to whet his appetite.

'Eat something,' Nadja urged. Her plate sat empty too. She tapped a notepad on the table beside her. 'I've started a list of things we have to cancel. Just add to it if anything comes to mind.'

'What do we have to cancel?'

'Mum's hair appointments, for one thing. She told me she'd booked her haircuts all the way to Christmas.'

Josef nodded and gazed over Nadja's shoulder at the to-do list attached to the fridge door. A miniscule Berlin TV Tower held the paper in place by one corner while an orange starfish magnet that one of the grandchildren had made secured the other side. He still remembered the night Eva had printed off that list . . .

He had just fixed himself a coffee when Eva waltzed into the kitchen with a satisfied grin on her face.

'What's that?' he asked her, pointing to the piece of paper she was brandishing.

'This, my darling, is a list of things to do before we die. See.' She held up the paper to show him.

'That's very morbid,' he said, reading the title. Eva had written "Twenty-Five Things To Do Before We Die" at the top of the page and, beneath, had listed out activities from walking the walls surrounding Dubrovnik's old town to seeing the Northern Lights.

'We took a new delivery of books today and there was a title in there called *One Hundred Things To Do Before You Die*. It inspired me to create our own list.'

'And you're starting with just twenty-five things?'

Eva laughed. 'It's quite a list already. Honestly, I wasn't sure we would have time to add much more to it.'

Josef scanned the activities. 'I might create my own list. I'm not sure I fancy number twenty-one – eating oysters.'

Eva snatched the paper from his hand. 'Oh, we don't need to do that. Turns out most of my ideas require travel so I had to add a few local activities.'

'Yes, because Berlin is famous for its oysters.'

Eva chose two magnets from the twenty or so they had

displayed and attached the list to their fridge door. 'You can scoff all you like, Mr Fischer, but when we're on our death bed, you'll be grateful I made us this list.'

Josef now counted thirteen items crossed off from the list of twenty-five. Fourteen, if he counted the cruise. Eva had been on a cruise with three friends at the end of last year but she'd said she wasn't scoring it off the list until she had been on a cruise with him. It wasn't Josef's idea of a holiday. He wasn't sure he had sea legs and feared that he'd hate the experience so much he would book a flight home as soon as they reached their first stop. Eva had said she would take that chance. Her patience and perseverance had paid off and they were due to set sail at the end of the month.

A tapping on the front door jolted Josef from his thoughts of the cruise Eva would never make it on.

'That'll be the funeral director, Dad. I'll get it.' A weariness had crept into Nadja's voice with the passing of the hours. 'Please be nice.'

He had never had to organise a funeral before – not even for his parents. His sisters had taken care of everything and had just told him where to be and when. Josef abandoned his lunch, held his fingers to his closed eyes for a few seconds, and moved back to the living room.

'Hello, I'm Lilli Meyer,' Josef heard the new arrival say from the hallway as he took his usual seat. Introducing herself was a better start, at least.

'I'm Nadja, Eva's daughter. Thank you for coming.'

'I'm so sorry for your loss, Nadja.'

'Thank you.'

Josef appraised the woman as she entered his home. Her shoulder-length blonde hair framed her face and he saw compassion in her eyes. She carried a black leather satchel and had a charcoal-coloured coat draped over her arm. Her grey trousers and lilac sweater presented a calm energy around her.

'Mr Fischer, I'm sorry for your loss. My name is Lilli and, with your permission, I'd like to take your wife into my care and take responsibility for any arrangements we have to make.'

Nadja sniffed and slumped onto the sofa.

Lilli put her coat and bag down on the opposite end of the sofa. She picked up the tray of coffee that had long since gone cold. 'I'll start by refreshing this coffee, shall I?'

Josef could only nod.

2

IN THE DAYS THAT FOLLOWED, LILLI HAD PROVED HERSELF TO be an unwavering support to Josef and Nadja. Her gentle suggestions and superior organisational skills had helped the Fischer family through their darkest days. She'd even taken on the task of locating and arranging the delivery of Diane's luggage when the airline lost track of it somewhere between Singapore and Berlin.

Diane, the youngest of the Fischer children, had broken down in uncontrollable sobs when the courier appeared at their front door with her two suitcases. Josef suspected Diane had been holding it all in since Nadja's initial call. He knew she would have immediately arranged flights, packed her bags and headed to the airport, a familiar routine for his travel-writer daughter. The wave of emotion had to crash through her barriers at some point and had chosen the arrival of her luggage as the time to do it.

Nadja had taken some time off from her accountancy firm – a perk of owning the company, she'd said. She spent her freed-up days working with Lilli, digging out family photos for use during the funeral service, shuffling paperwork and condolences cards and making lists. Her list of things to cancel had apparently spread onto a second page in her notebook.

Mark and Sebastian had arrived from Luxembourg and Stuttgart, whereupon Sebastian spent most of his time pacing around the kitchen on work calls having roped Diane into organising flights and a hotel for his wife, their teenaged twin girls and their elder son. The distraction was good for her, and she had offered to book a hotel for Mark, too; however, his two teenaged boys seemed to like camping on the floor of their father's old bedroom. Mark handed them a wad of cash each morning and they happily made themselves scarce until dinnertime. At fifteen and sixteen years old, they relished the temporary freedom.

Having all of his children and grandchildren in his house at the same time only happened once every three or four years, for Christmas, when their schedules and wider family commitments lined up. He and Eva had hosted Christmas only last year and they had gone all out with the celebrations for three full days. Eva had remarked that it would probably be the last year they were all together at the same time. Nadja's eyes had widened and she'd looked at Josef as though expecting bad news. His eldest child had three strong personality traits: a fiery temper, a quick wit, and a tendency to worry.

'Relax,' he'd said. 'No one is dying. Although I don't appreciate you assuming I'll be the first to go.'

Nadja laughed and stretched her legs out to rest her feet on the coffee table. 'Reduce that pregnant-looking belly if you want to change that assumption,' she quipped.

Eva smiled at the giggling from their youngest grandchildren huddled together in the corner of the room. She tapped Josef's stomach. 'You can't blame my cooking for that. It's all pastry in there. I just mean that the children are all getting older. They'll want to have Christmas with their friends, and with boyfriends and girlfriends, soon.'

Nadja nodded. 'Three of the children are now officially in their twenties. I'm not sure how that happened.'

'Time only speeds up,' Josef said.

Then the kitchen timer had beeped and Eva, moving forwards on her chair, had announced: 'On that cheery note, lunch is ready.'

Josef was now grateful that they'd had their last family Christmas, even though they were wrong about why it was the last one. They had been free to enjoy their time together, spoil their children and grandchildren, and gorge on glorious food without the weight of ill health and loss bearing down on them.

When the day of Eva's funeral arrived, Josef was exhausted from the constant noise and the handful of questions and orders that were recycled at least a few times every hour. *Are you OK, Dad? Can I get you something, Dad? Are you hungry, Dad? You sit still, Dad, I'll do that for you.*

He knew he should be grateful to have family around him at this time, and he was, but he also longed for a few minutes of peace and quiet in the day to grieve for the woman he had spent almost every day with since they were both fifteen years old.

Fleeting rain showers pattered on the windows throughout the morning and occasional gusts of wind howled under the front door. The commotion in the house ground to a halt as everyone crept around on their tiptoes as though any noise was disrespectful on the morning of a funeral.

Josef arrived at the church to a recording of violins playing the melody of 'Somewhere Over the Rainbow'. He had requested the song at the end of the service, as Eva had wanted. Lilli must have arranged for the tune to be played at the start, too. It was a nice touch. Eva would have liked it.

Eva's dark wooden casket, adorned with white lilies and deep-red roses, rested at the front of the church. Josef settled into the first row of seating, flanked by his four children. He had overheard a conversation between Nadja and Lilli about high-gloss or matt caskets. He saw now that they had opted for high-gloss with rectangular panels framing polished brass handles. The more he stared at the casket, the more certain he became that Eva wasn't in it. In the stillness, the only noise being people shifting in their seats on the wooden benches and the soft music, he sensed a familiarity around him that wasn't the proximity of his children. A tingle crossed his shoulder blades and he chose to believe it was his Eva.

Josef sat through the service and listened to the pastor telling stories of his wife and their life together. She talked about all that Eva had crammed into her seventy-one years, her fierce love for her family, her adventurous spirit.

Where Josef was calm and considered, Eva had been bold and impulsive. It was a combination that didn't always work in a marriage, but it had for them. Eva had learned to recognise when she needed to take a step back and think things through and Josef had become accustomed to his wife prodding him to take the less cautious approach on occasion. Perfectly balanced, Eva had called them.

The pastor captured Eva's spirit in the stories she told. She'd been a ball of happiness from when she bounced out of bed in the morning until she turned in at night. It was a character trait that had served her well in her first occupation as full-time caregiver to their four children and then in her later career as the manager of an independent department store.

The pastor talked about Eva's particular pride in the children's department she had created. There were no signs telling the little ones not to touch. Instead, there was a wide-open space in the middle of the floor with an abundance of toys for children to try. A train set circled the perimeter overhead and building blocks, doll's houses, mechanical animals and musical instruments were unboxed and ready for play. Dive right in and experience life – that's how Eva lived and how she encouraged those around her to live.

Nadja's arm brushed against Josef's as it twitched with her silent sobs and he reached his hand out to still her trembling. Mark wiped tears away from his eyes with the navy-blue handkerchief he'd tucked into the top pocket of his suit. Josef placed a hand on his son's knee and Mark gripped his hand in a way he hadn't done since he was a boy. Seeing the impact of Eva's death on his children gave him an ache in his chest. Tears pricked his own eyes as he mourned for their loss.

He glanced down and saw the order of service Nadja clutched in her other hand with Eva's face beaming from the page. He remembered the day the photograph had been taken. It was last summer and they'd held a picnic in the park to celebrate Nadja's daughter's graduation. Josef wasn't much of a photographer but seeing the pride, happiness and love on his wife's face that day had compelled him to pick up their camera and capture her image. Her eyes had met the camera lens at just the right moment for him to immortalise the glint in them.

The melody of 'Somewhere Over the Rainbow' drifted into his consciousness again – a guitar, a piano, the upbeat melody and the flawless voice of the singer. It was Eva's version. He listened to the words. A tear rolled down his cheek and Josef grieved for his wife and for what he, too, had lost.

3
____

It had been two days since Eva's funeral and the house had yet to quieten down. Partners and children had travelled home the day before but Josef's own children still hovered over him. They had fashioned makeshift desks out of all manner of random surfaces in the house; Diane was using a dressing table upstairs and Mark was occupying the window sill in the living room, his laptop overhanging the edge as he perched in front of it on one of the wooden chairs from the kitchen. The four of his children hadn't spent this long in the same house since they were teenagers. Josef had insisted that they all make plans to go back to their own homes, but no one seemed to be leaving – not even Diane, who had literally made it her life's work not to stay in the same place for too long.

Nadja sat with Sebastian on the sofa opposite Josef and opened the mail. She held up a magazine in clear plastic wrapping. 'It's mum's travel magazine. I'll add it to the list of things to cancel.'

Eva had scampered to the letterbox every month when her magazine arrived. She'd fold over the pages of the destinations she wanted to go to and would add an extra fold to the bottom corner of any pages that featured a place she thought Josef would like too.

Nadja scribbled something on her notepad and tossed it, along with the unopened magazine, onto the coffee table. Josef scanned the cover headlines for destinations that might have caught Eva's eye. His gaze settled on 'The Ultimate Guide to Solo Travel'. Eva should have been sitting here reading that article and listening to Nadja churn out all of the reasons why she couldn't travel on her own. It wasn't Eva's time to go. It should have been him.

Josef picked up the notepad and scanned Nadja's list. Unsurprisingly, the recurring word that jumped out at him was *cancel*. Not only was she cancelling Eva's magazine subscriptions, she was also cancelling her mobile phone, their upcoming cruise and their weekend on Sylt in August.

Sylt was one of the places Eva had been considering for a move. It suited their mutual wish to be by the sea, but it wasn't a serious contender. Eva had worried it might be too touristy for her liking and Josef had had his own reservations when he'd looked at house prices on the island. A cosy little cottage with a garden and a sea view was out of the question – their budget would barely stretch to an upper-level apartment that looked directly into the neighbour's living room.

Josef inspected the list again. Nadja was also, for a reason he couldn't fathom, cancelling their television package. Eva did love to watch an afternoon movie with coffee and a cake, but he was partial to the odd TV show himself and, with Eva gone, he'd have more time on his hands, not less.

'Dad, are you selling the house?'

Josef looked up and saw Nadja holding a large white envelope with a stack of papers.

'We were,' he said. It was a contract that he had signed and attached copies of his identity documents to. The real-estate agent had visited the house the week before Eva's death. He'd taken photographs and explained his fees. All he needed was for them to sign and return the paperwork and their house would be listed for sale. Eva hadn't cared that they didn't have anywhere else to go to yet; she'd just wanted to get the process started and had said a quick sale would give them the momentum they needed to get serious about their property search.

'But why would you sell?' Nadja asked.

'You know we wanted to move to the coast,' said Josef.

'Oh, right. I didn't realise you had set things in motion.' She shuffled the papers and slipped them back into the envelope. 'There's still plenty of time to cancel that.'

Cancel. There was that word again.

'We don't need to cancel,' Mark chipped in from his workspace at the front of the room. 'I know we haven't decided who Dad will live with yet, but we need to sell this place regardless.'

Josef couldn't help but wonder if *he* was part of the *we* that had yet to make that decision. The children meant well – of course they did – but there were some decisions that were his to make. He just needed a bit of space to think through his options. He dug his palms into the arms of his chair and pushed himself up. When Sebastian sprung up from his own chair and gripped Josef's arm, he brushed him off. 'I'm just going for a walk. I need the fresh air.'

The children all looked at each other and Josef knew they were silently working out which one of them was going to accompany him.

'Let me grab my coat,' said Sebastian. 'I'll come with you.'

Josef shook his head. 'No need. I'm perfectly fine wandering about on my own.'

'I know you are, Dad. But, honestly, I could use the fresh air myself.' Sebastian picked up Josef's coat and held it out for him to slip on. Once Josef's arms were in the sleeves, his son straightened out the collar and Josef half expected to be spun around and have his coat zipped up. Instead, Sebastian gave him a smile and hauled his own coat on, then opened the front door.

A welcome air rushed around Josef as he stepped out onto the street. His head was fuzzy from both the constant surveillance and the central heating that one of the children had found it necessary to have on every hour of the day.

It was no good. He needed his house back. And he needed the space to miss Eva if he was ever going to move on to the next stage of grief, whatever that was supposed to be.

4

———

JOSEF PLUNGED HIS HANDS INTO A BOWL CF FLOUR, WATER, yeast and salt and mixed the ingredients together. Diane had left first thing that morning to catch her flight back to Singapore. He hadn't yet been able to get his other three children to leave his house, but he had been able to get them out of his kitchen. His fingers massaged the emerging dough and the knots across his shoulders released with each rhythmic movement.

Once his dough had come together, he covered the bowl and set it aside. He sprinkled a touch of flour across his worktop and uncovered a bowl of dough he had prepared earlier. He pressed his fist into the dough to deflate the air pockets and tipped it onto the floured surface. Using the expert eye he had honed over fifty years of baking, Josef formed eight equal-sized buns.

The letterbox clanged at the other side of the house and he knew Nadja would be on her feet within seconds to scoop up whatever had been delivered. He smiled when his daughter appeared at the kitchen door with an arm full of mail. Eva had generally handled their post and flagged anything that needed his attention, but he didn't remember there ever being so many letters. The volume of sympathy cards arriving for him had now diminished so the bundle Nadja was holding must have been something to do with the heavy administrative burden that seemed to accompany a death.

Managing the paperwork had become Nadja's preferred way of keeping herself busy while virtually living in his house and, honestly, he was happy to let her do it. When his bank had accidentally frozen his access to the joint account, he had experienced first hand how frustrating it was to notify an organisation of a person's death. Considering that people die every day, he found the lack of procedures – and empathy – astonishing. He didn't mind admitting that the admin side of things would have overwhelmed him.

Nadja plonked herself down on a chair at the kitchen table and was swiftly followed by Mark, carrying takeaway coffees.

'What are you making, Dad?' Mark asked, waving a cup of coffee above the worktop as he searched for a spot that wasn't covered in flour.

'Baguettes and brioche buns.' Josef stretched out a dough-covered hand and took the coffee. A comforting heat from the cup radiated up his arm. He removed the lid and took a gulp, closely followed by another one. Eva used to say that coffee tasted better when someone else made it for you. He teased her that it was just her way of getting him to make the coffee, but she had a point. He took another swig of the hot, black liquid and for a moment imagined Eva standing in the doorway telling him to get the kitchen tidied up.

Josef covered his buns for a final proving and washed the surfaces, trying to drown out the chatter between his children.

'Of course, he could move in with any one of us, but it makes most sense for it to be Sebastian,' Mark was saying.

'Oh, for goodness' sake,' Nadja huffed. She tossed an envelope across the table towards Mark. 'I can't get anyone in that travel company to phone me back and now they've sent out the tickets.'

Mark picked up the envelope and peered inside. 'What tickets?'

'The cruise I've been trying to cancel all week. I can't be the first person to cancel a holiday, but no one seems to know what to do about it.'

Josef bristled at their conversation.

Mark slipped the tickets out of the envelope. 'I'll call them today and insist they escalate the request to a manager. So, we're agreed that Dad should go to live with Sebastian?'

Nadja nodded. 'That sounds good, doesn't it, Dad?'

Josef had heard that tone before. It was the tone Nadja used on her children when she was telling them what to do while trying to make it sound as though they had a choice. 'I'm not going to live with Sebastian.'

'You'll enjoy it once you're there,' said Nadja. 'Seb has a spare bedroom with its own bathroom and the girls are heading to university after the summer so there's plenty of space.'

Josef wiped the last of the flour and dough remnants into his cupped hand and tossed them into the sink. 'I don't want to move to Stuttgart'.

'That's fine,' said Nadja. 'You'll stay with me, then.'

He dried his hands and leaned forward on the counter. 'I'll stay here. I'm not completely helpless.'

'But, Dad . . .'

'But, nothing,' he said, cutting her off. 'I'm perfectly capable of living on my own.'

'We know you are, Dad,' said Mark, his tone soft for a change. 'But why would you want to do that when you could be around family?'

He didn't know if he wanted to be. That was the point. He had barely spent an hour alone since waking up on that dreadful morning to find his Eva was no longer here.

'I appreciate the offer, Nadja, but I'm not going to stay with you, either.'

'OK. Where do you want to go?'

'The first place I'm going is Hamburg, and then we'll see.'

Nadja and Mark exchanged glances. Mark shrugged. 'What do you mean?'

Josef strode to the table and snatched up the envelope. 'I'm going on this cruise.' The confines of a cabin on a cruise ship would give him more breathing space than he currently had in his three-bedroomed home.

5

Five days after stunning his children into silence in his kitchen, Josef was in Hamburg with the spring sunshine beating down on his back. He was grateful he'd remembered to pack a hat, the rim of which now kept his neck from burning. His elder daughter crouched for the third time to check his luggage tag was still secure.

'The ship is huge, Dad.' Nadja rose and craned her neck skyward to take in the eight-storey ship towering above them as they stood on the viewing platform.

The upper decks of the ship comprised six storeys of glass-fronted balconies. It looked like a beachfront hotel if you averted your eyes from the pale blue metal hull and the word 'Liberty', painted in letters that were likely taller than Josef. The Liberty sat on the rippling water as the sunshine gave the sea a sparkle perfect for the photos that were being taken by scores of passengers as they waited to board.

'I hope the weather stays good if that's how much the boat rocks on a calm sea,' said Josef. Rocking was perhaps a bit of an exaggeration, but given the size of the ship, it was surreal to see it moving at all. They had been told to keep an eye on the weather and prepare for choppier waters. Eva hadn't seen this as a problem – she'd told Josef they would be off the ship all day and asleep for most of the sailing time. Still, he was grateful for the sunshine and what looked to be as calm a sea as he could expect at this time of year.

'I still can't believe you're going on this cruise,' Nadja said.

'Your mother wanted to cruise the North Sea cities. She wanted to soak up some history rather than sunshine for a change.' Eva had hoped to wander cobbled streets and see picturesque canals without hordes of tourists getting in the way. That's why she'd chosen the end of April and a cruise that would take them from Hamburg to Southampton, France, Belgium and Amsterdam. She wanted to avoid the summer months and she feared any later in the year would be too cold and wet for them to enjoy their time off the ship.

'But she's not here to experience it.' Nadja's clipped tone softened. 'You're still grieving, Dad.'

'I can grieve in my living room or grieve on a cruise ship. Which do you think your mother would prefer?' He was proud of the certainty in his question. He knew the answer, and Nadja knew it too.

Nadja laughed and shook her head. She knew as well as he did that Eva would have approved of him taking the cruise. Eva was a woman whose enthusiasm for each stage of her life and work had never waned and she had carried that same enthusiasm into her retirement.

Like her mother, Nadja spoke her mind, but that was where their similarities ended. The most anxious of his children, Nadja prioritised safety over adventure, and waving her elderly – in her opinion – father off on a cruise on his own would be a struggle for her. He *knew* it was a struggle for her. But the ticket was booked and Josef's cabin was awaiting him; all he had to do was walk into the terminal and officially check in.

Nadja insisted on accompanying Josef into the terminal at his allotted time and he knew she would remain right by his side until the security protocols prevented her from going a step further. They dropped his luggage off with the porters, headed into the terminal and joined the queue. There were easily a hundred people in front of them, all shuffling their way towards the check-in desks. Within only a quarter of an hour, another hundred or so people had appeared behind them.

A young man with short dark hair and a neatly pressed navy-blue uniform made his way steadily along the queue, scanning tickets and answering questions as he went. Adam, according to his brass name badge, was much taller than Josef – although that wasn't hard these days, given how fast Josef seemed to be shrinking. No one mentioned old-age shrinking. They talked about the aches and pains, the forgetfulness, the calling your children two or three different names before landing on the right one, but Josef didn't remember anyone preparing him for how he would lose inches as he gained years.

'Can I scan your tickets, please?' Adam spoke German words but with a detectable English accent.

Josef glimpsed a ball of chewing gum in the man's mouth as he handed his printed ticket across. 'Should you be chewing that gum at work?' he asked him in English.

Adam's cheeks flushed and he glanced over his shoulder towards a woman with a tight bun in her hair and a severe look on her face. 'I'm sorry, sir. No, I shouldn't be. I'm trying to stop smoking and the gum takes the edge off.'

Josef nodded. 'That's an admirable goal. Keep it going.'

Adam exhaled and his shoulders sagged. He scanned

the ticket and the screen on his small device lit up green. 'Ah, you're in the wrong queue, sir.'

Josef removed his hat and fanned himself with it. 'Nadja, you should just go. This might take a while.'

'Actually, sir, it won't.' Adam pointed at the letters on the corner of Josef's ticket. 'PB means priority boarding. Your queue is that short one over there.'

Josef looked at the other queue. Seven people stood beneath a Priority Boarding banner and they looked like one family. The two young children, a boy and a girl, chased each other around the group of grown-ups, and a teenaged boy perched on top of a suitcase on wheels – one of those sturdy ones made from hard plastic – with chunky white headphones covering his ears. The parents, and presumably the grandparents if they were indeed all together, huddled around another Adam lookalike who was scanning their tickets.

'If you show my colleague over there your ticket, he'll get you all set up to board. Thank you for sailing with us. Enjoy your holiday, sir.'

Josef and Nadja thanked Adam and left the queue of hundreds to join the queue of seven. He should have known Eva would've booked priority boarding. That had been her one complaint when she'd returned from the cruise earlier in the year – it had taken over an hour for her to board. Wasted wine time, she had called it. She'd said they should organise entry as they did for flights by inviting those that need assistance to board first. They didn't actually need assistance, but she saw speedy boarding for holidays and almost always guaranteed seats on the Berlin S-Bahn as a perk of advancing years.

Adam's colleague rescanned Josef's ticket, took his photograph and ran through the various timings that Josef needed to know, including when he could access his room and what time the ship would set sail. He gestured towards the security scanners for hand luggage and pointed out the terminal exit for boarding directly onto the ship.

Josef thanked the steward and glanced at his watch, having paid particular attention to the entry time for his room. Not long to wait.

Nadja took Josef's ticket and slipped it into the clear plastic wallet she had prepared containing his travel documents, insurance details, family telephone numbers and emergency-contact numbers for each country on the cruise route. She handed him the folder and repeated the speech she'd given him before they left Berlin. 'I've also included work telephone numbers for me, Mark and Seb, just in case. No point calling Diane – she's too far away,' she concluded.

Josef tugged at the edges of his coat and made a show of scrutinising the inside lining. 'And have you stitched my name and address inside my coat in case I get lost?'

Nadja's face fell.

Josef smiled and put a hand on her shoulder. 'Relax. I know you think I'm a dithering old man, but I'm a grown-up. I can travel on my own and ask for help if I need it.'

'Oh, Dad, you're not a *dithering* old man.'

Josef laughed at the glint in her eye and emphasis on the word dithering. 'Just old, then.'

She shrugged. 'No point pretending otherwise.'

'Don't wait for the ship to leave. Get to your hotel before it gets too late.'

Nadja nodded. It was too far for her to drive back to Berlin tonight. The ship didn't leave for hours yet and Josef didn't want her hanging around the docks on her own. He plastered on what he hoped was his most reassuring grin and said his goodbyes, but Nadja was unable to hide her concern.

Once on board, and doing his best to ignore excitable passengers squealing and taking photographs, Josef took the opportunity to explore the ship while he waited for access to his room. He headed up the escalator and onto the main deck, or the atrium as it was called on his map. He hadn't realised the ship would be big enough to require a map for navigation. It was so long that he couldn't see from one end to the other, yet when he closed his eyes he felt himself swaying. It was a swaying he probably wouldn't even have noticed had he been wandering along with Eva chattering in his ear. How could it be that a structure this enormous didn't feel stable on the water?

The atrium was a mass of people checking out restaurants for possible dinner options or having a drink at one of the twelve bars on board while waiting for their rooms. Josef figured if he kept moving then he wouldn't feel the vibration of the ship. The cruise had been Eva's idea, not his, and he didn't want anything to put him off going before the ship had even left the port.

When Eva had returned from her cruise around Spain and Portugal, she'd told him the scale of the ship was like nothing she could have imagined. She'd said it wasn't like being in a hotel, it was like being in a small town. He saw that now as he weaved through hundreds of people sauntering along a wide walkway lined with palm trees in pots that were at least half the height of Josef and just as wide. He approached a spiral staircase that climbed towards a glass dome, crowded with passengers taking photographs, at the very top of the ship. Circling underneath it, he headed back along the atrium.

After almost an hour of wandering back and forth, Josef arrived at his ocean-view room with a balcony. He unlatched the glass door, slid it open, and stepped onto his balcony for some fresh air. A deep breath filled his throat with an unfamiliar mix of salty air and diesel, which he really hoped was coming from the cargo ships and wasn't an odour that would linger for the entire cruise. Despite the warmth he'd felt from the sunshine while on the dock, the air around his balcony was chilly. He headed back inside, slid his door closed and slumped on the sofa, one of the four seating options in his suite. Eva had selected full-on luxury.

It was dark by the time the ship set sail. Footsteps passed his cabin door as fellow passengers explored the ship and made their way to their first dinner at sea. Josef had eaten with Nadja before he boarded and had no desire to explore anything tonight.

The next nine days would give him his first experience of being truly alone. The boys and Diane had returned home earlier in the week but Nadja had taken up residence in his house to *help out*, she said. To keep an eye on him was a more accurate description. He appreciated her support, but he had to deal with his new reality at some point. Prolonging it further was only prolonging his grief. It wasn't that he was ready to say goodbye to Eva. He would never be ready to do that. Eva believed in living life, and avoiding reality wasn't living.

Josef stood up and glanced at his unopened suitcase, conveniently placed by the crew on the table near the wardrobe. He pulled back the crisp white sheets, crawled into the king-size bed and sank into a fitful sleep.

6

─────────

JOSEF POPPED ANOTHER COFFEE POD IN THE MACHINE – HIS third that morning. The machine screeched into action and released a velvet liquid into the small blue cup that he had cradled since wakening. He unlatched his cabin door and stepped onto the forward-facing balcony. Given the size of his suite and position of the balcony, Eva must have opted for one of the most expensive rooms on the ship.

He sat on a deckchair on his balcony and placed his coffee on the table, keeping his gaze fixed on the vast ocean on the other side of the glass barrier and not on the empty deckchair beside him. A sea view was why Eva had been talking of moving out of the city and heading to the coast: she said they had served their time in the city; they had raised their children there and seen them settled into their careers, with their own families; now, she wanted to wander quiet streets, breathe seaside air and live somewhere their grandchildren would love to visit for holidays.

With the vast ocean in front of him and the only sound being the cruise liner powering its way through the waves many floors beneath him, Josef had never felt so isolated. He abandoned his coffee, pulled his cabin door closed behind him and made his way to the nearest lift.

The first bar Josef encountered that didn't have a crowd of people waiting to enter was more opulent than he had expected. The bar featured dark green leather stools and chairs and immaculately polished brass fixtures and fittings. A solo pianist played soft music at a grand piano on a small stage in the back corner of the bar. The stands and microphones around her suggested a fuller band would appear at some point in the evening. Josef didn't know much about decor but from the design of the bar, he suspected this was what would be called a gentlemen's club.

Despite Eva's descriptions, he had been expecting life on board a cruise ship to be akin to that he'd experienced on the short ferry rides he'd taken over the years. He had envisaged orange plastic chairs bolted onto a damp floor, and narrow passageways with metal railings for steadying himself in rough seas. Instead, his cabin featured a luxurious carpet, Egyptian cotton sheets, a full-sized bath and fluffy towels that were softer than the ones he had at home.

Josef hoisted himself onto the only vacant bar stool and ordered a beer. He wrapped his hand around the glass, condensation seeping between his fingers, and raised the drink to the man on his left. 'Cheers,' he said.

The man beside him raised his own glass with not much more than froth nestled in the bottom. 'Cheers. I'll take another, please,' he said to the bartender.

Josef looked again at the man. 'I think I saw you before we left the port. You're travelling with two young children and a teenager, right?'

The man smiled and nodded. 'My grandchildren. We're here with my son and his wife.'

Although it had been the children that caught Josef's

eye, he'd seen enough of the adults to recognise the man straight away given that the queue for priority boarding had been so short. The man was similar in age and build to Josef only he didn't have the growing pastry paunch that Josef had.

'I'm Josef. The younger ones seem very lively. They'll keep you on your toes.'

The man laughed and thanked the bartender for his refreshed beer. 'I'm Bernhard. And yes, lively is a good word for those two. They're twins. Just turned four.'

'Ah. That's a good age.' Josef took a gulp of his beer. He would never have wished away the childhood of his grandchildren but he was grateful that the youngest of them were now teenagers. He was even more grateful that they were teenagers who'd retained the happy chattiness that had been with them since their younger days. Nadja's youngest was now thirteen – one of the reasons Eva felt ready to move away from Berlin. Babysitting duties had declined over the last couple of years and it was their time once again, she had said.

'Have you been on a cruise before?' asked Bernhard.

Josef shook his head and took another gulp of his beer. 'My first one. You?'

'My fifth. I love being able to wander about the holiday resort knowing I can't get lost for too long.' Bernhard chuckled and raised his glass. 'Although there are definite advantages to getting lost for at least a bit.'

'Bernhard!' bellowed a voice from behind. Josef steadied his glass as if expecting the reverberation to knock it over.

Bernhard looked at Josef, raised his eyebrows and forced a smile. 'It seems I've been found.'

Josef turned and came face to face with the older woman

who had been with Bernhard on the docks. His wife, presumably.

'The children are waiting for lunch and you're here filling yourself up on beer.' The woman pointed her finger inches from Bernhard's face. 'You had better eat your lunch after this. Come on.'

A chastised Bernhard took a final gulp of his beer and skulked out of the bar behind his wife, giving Josef a wave as he went.

Josef winced. Eva was a woman not short of opinions, but she would never have spoken so brutally to him. Not even behind closed doors.

'Can I get you another?' The bartender pointed at Josef's glass, which was already half empty.

'No, thank you. I would like to eat, though. Do you have any recommendations?' When he still had the bakery, he was up and working before dawn. Breakfast was a meal that happened some hours after leaving his warm bed. A glance at his watch now told him he had left his bed seven hours ago and all he'd had was three coffees and half a beer.

The bartender plucked a menu from beneath the bar and set it in front of Josef. 'Our rib-eye burger is excellent if you're looking for something classic. Or you can try the speciality seafood restaurant next door. We have almost every cuisine on board – what type of food do you like?'

'A rib-eye burger sounds like just the thing.'

'Good choice. Are you sure I can't get you another drink while you wait?'

Josef shook his head. 'I think I'll stretch my legs. Shall we say thirty minutes?'

'Certainly. I'll have a table ready for you when you get back.'

Josef thanked the bartender and left the subtle piano

music behind as he strolled towards a crowd of people that had gathered near the spiral staircase at the end of the ship's atrium.

'What's happening here?' he asked a woman who was standing on her tiptoes to see towards the front of the crowd.

'It's photos with the captain,' she said as she kept her gaze fixed in front of her and wobbled forwards.

Josef turned at the distinctive sound of flip-flops and saw a young couple with beach towels over their arms ignoring the crowd and heading towards a narrower set of stairs. He followed the couple, making his way past the messy queue of people hoping to meet the captain, and paused at the foot of the stairs, where a sign on the wall directed 'To pool deck'. Josef was about to go up the stairs when he caught sight of the captain flanked by two men and a little girl with what looked to be a professional photographer capturing the moment. The girl was only half the height of the captain and she gazed up adoringly at the impressive woman before her. The captain wore the traditional blue blazer with gold stripes on her cuffs and her blonde hair poked out from beneath her peaked cap. Once the photo had been taken, the captain knelt down and exchanged a few words with the beaming girl.

Josef put one foot on the stairs then paused again. Eva would have made him stand in line to get their photograph taken with the captain.

'Not today, darling,' he mumbled. He gripped the handrail and made his way up to the pool deck.

There was a wall of people on the other side of a set of glass doors and the distinctive smell of chlorine leached out from the pool area. Josef immediately decided to keep going up. The last staircase brought him out into the fresh air high above the waves. He wandered over to the barrier in the centre of the ship and stared down at the white froth bubbling up at one end of the swimming pool. He shuddered at the human soup below him. There must have been fifty or so people in the pool and quite literally hundreds lying side by side on sunbeds. He presumed there was some on-deck heating because the April sunshine didn't feel warm enough to explain the amount of flesh on show beneath him.

As he walked alongside the outer railing, the occasional mist of water cooled the air further. His stomach grumbled in protest against his long morning with no food and he stepped onto the escalator at the end of the deck, ready to quieten the rumble with a rib-eye burger.

Back in the atrium, another commotion caught his eye. The captain had gone but a small crowd of people had remained and now gathered in a circle. Josef weaved his way to the front of the huddle to see two of the ship's crew kneeling down. One crewmember spoke into a radio while the other loosened the shirt collar of the man Josef had been speaking with only half an hour earlier.

Bernhard was on the ground, propped up against a pillar. He clutched his chest, his face contorted with pain and his eyes turning red right in front of Josef. His wife rummaged in her handbag and passed something to one of the crew.

Josef's skin prickled. He touched his neck where his pulse was now thudding and looked away. Whatever was about to happen to his shipmate, it wasn't something that required spectators. He pushed his way through the growing crowd, his appetite suddenly gone.

7

THE FOLLOWING DAY THE SHIP HAD DOCKED IN SOUTHAMPTON before Josef was even awake. He took a coffee onto the balcony and browsed the recommended things to do in his cabin literature. One of the photographs on a leaflet showed a street sign confirming that buses, taxis and trains could all be accessed within just a few minutes of the terminal for those requiring onward travel.

Eva had already booked them on an excursion to the city of Bath for today – two hours on a coach, lunch in Bath, then another two-hour journey back to the ship – and tomorrow morning he would wake up in Le Havre, where, according to the notes Nadja had printed out for him, he would travel to the Normandy landing beaches. Cities with history, cobbled streets, canals – that had been Eva's plan. He was torn between following Eva's itinerary and responding to the gnawing feeling in his gut that told him to abandon the ship and head straight to Heathrow Airport.

Or there was another option. He could take a train north. It had been decades since he'd travelled from London to Edinburgh.

He looked down again at the leaflet in his hand. The barman had told him that Bernhard and his family would be leaving the ship as soon as they docked. He knew that Bernhard was alive, but he didn't know anything more than that. Eva had gone to sleep at night and hadn't woken up in the morning. That had been it. No warning. No illness to prepare those left behind. He couldn't help but wonder – if they had known, would they have spent their time differently this last year?

Of course, it was a question that had no answer. He couldn't possibly know what they would have chosen to do with a bit of advance warning. The children would've fussed over them more than they already did, that's for sure. And Eva would have worried about him. Would that have been worse? Could anything have been worse than the pain he'd experienced these last few weeks?

Josef stood up and heaved his suitcase onto the bed. His cruise had come to an end. He packed his belongings, zipped his suitcase closed, grabbed his smaller bag and strode towards the exit.

Arriving at the place where he'd boarded, Josef looked around him. There were plenty of people strolling around and a handful of crewmembers mingling, but the double doors were still closed and there was no obvious way out.

A crewmember caught Josef's eye and made his way towards him. 'Can I help you with something, sir?'

'Yes. Can you tell me where to get off?'

The man's friendly gaze roamed over Josef's suitcase and the bag he was lugging with him. 'Passengers are not yet permitted to disembark. Do you have an excursion booked with us?'

Josef nodded. 'I do, but I won't be on it. I need to get to Heathrow.'

The man put his hand on Josef's elbow and steered him back the way he had just come. 'I'll take you to the main reception desk first. They'll be able to advise you on the disembarkation process and cancel the rest of your trip, if necessary.'

Josef followed and sighed as he realised leaving the cruise was likely to be harder than actually getting on it. 'Will this take long?'

'Another hour or so. We just have some procedures to follow before we can allow passengers to leave. Security, customs checks, things like that. May I ask why you're leaving?'

It was a perfectly reasonable question with an answer that Josef didn't know how to articulate. As if sensing the answer wasn't something Josef wanted to give, his escort switched to a more practical question. 'What time is your flight?'

Josef froze. Once he arrived at the airport, he could be back in Berlin in less than two hours. He wasn't sure that would be any better. He didn't want to stay on the ship, but he wasn't yet ready to return home either. There were far too many people trying to steer him in directions he didn't think he wanted to go in.

He pulled his suitcase into an upright position. 'Actually, I'm not going to the airport. I'm taking the train.'

Josef knew already that Nadja would be furious.

8

Two trains and a taxi ride later Josef was standing on the promenade of Thistle Bay, an hour north of Edinburgh, his suitcase at his feet. Clusters of stalls were sprawled along the promenade turning the quiet town he remembered into a bustling stretch of enterprise that wouldn't have looked out of place on the streets of Berlin.

The road had been closed to traffic for the day. People milled about chatting and eating food and Josef's stomach gurgled at the delicious scent of barbecued meat. Purple bunting was everywhere and the sound of fiddles, guitars and a female voice with a distinct Scottish twang filled the air as traditional folk music poured from a giant speaker nearby.

It had been decades since he'd last stood on this promenade and a surge of memories deluged his thoughts. He had been born only a few miles from the small Scottish coastal town and had been a regular visitor to this very beach during the first ten years of his life.

Josef smiled. He felt lighter than he had in days and he

was certain that Eva would have approved of his holiday alteration.

He dropped his luggage off at the local bed and breakfast, thankful he'd been able to get a last-minute check-in. Before going back out to explore, he put an extra jumper on under his coat. The temperature was a good few degrees cooler than he was used to at this time of year and it somehow felt colder in Thistle Bay than it had on the top deck of the Liberty.

He wandered into the heart of the street festival and perused the stalls. People were selling everything from handmade candles to musical instruments and dried seaweed. A craft-beer stall caught his eye and he glanced at his watch. He had left Southampton nine hours ago. It was certainly late enough for a beer, but he should really eat something first.

Josef followed his nose to the food stalls and caught sight of the chubby hand of a toddler helping herself to salami samples. Her parents were distracted swapping the stall owner a crisp ten-pound note for a brown paper bag with sticks of cured sausages poking out of the top. Josef smiled as he recalled joking with Eva about how they'd visited many festivals in many countries and had yet to find one that didn't have a German sausage stall.

The other half of the stall housed a large outdoor grill covered in skewered meat that gave off a mouth-watering aroma as it sizzled.

'Can I tempt you?' the man in charge of the grill asked in a pronounced Greek accent. 'Traditional lamb souvlaki with local lamb.'

'Yes, you can,' said Josef. 'It smells wonderful.'

The cook was a young man in his twenties, Josef estimated, with a mound of thick black hair that had been styled to look dishevelled. Nadja's eldest son had the same hairstyle and Josef knew it took him at least ten minutes of preening with hair wax every morning to achieve the look. The man batted away some of the smoke from the grill with one hand and grabbed a pitta bread with the other. He warmed the pitta on the grill for a few seconds then stuffed it with hot chunks of cooked lamb, tomatoes, onions and topped it off with a spoonful of a creamy dressing.

'Here you go,' he said, tucking the souvlaki into a sheet of greaseproof paper and handing it over. 'Enjoy!'

Josef gave him the cash for it. The tuna sandwich he'd eaten on the train hadn't satisfied his hunger for long and he took a ravenous bite. The juices from the meat combined with the rich spiced marinade to create a sensational burst of flavour that made Josef glad he'd waited so long to eat. 'Your cooking transports me back to Athens with just a single bite. Authentic Greek souvlaki cooked by an authentic Greek.'

'You've been to Greece?'

Josef nodded and took another bite. 'Only Athens. A long time ago.' He and Eva had gone for a wedding. They had stayed for a few days, but the flavour-packed food had created a lasting impression. He'd even added Greek-inspired bread with feta and olives to his bakery menu, which had proved to be very popular.

'You're German, right?'

'I am. Josef Fischer.'

'I'm Alex. He's Christos.' Christos waved from the other end of the stall where he was busy serving a growing line of customers seeking German sausages. 'If you like Greek food, you'll love my moussaka. We run the local pub – The Smugglers Inn.'

'That doesn't sound very Greek.'

Alex smiled and loaded more meat onto his grill. 'The pub was here long before us and it will be here long after we're gone, I suspect. You should stop by. How long are you in town for?'

'That is a good question, young man, and it's currently one I don't have an answer to.'

Alex raised a dark eyebrow and waited for Josef to explain.

'You could say I drifted here by accident.'

Alex shook his head. 'There are no accidents, my friend.'

He was right, in this case at least. Josef wasn't here by accident. He had sought out two trains and a taxi with this destination in mind. But why? Was it as simple as retreating to familiarity when life was tough? Familiarity was his home in Berlin. Thistle Bay was just a childhood memory.

'Moussaka at the pub for dinner tomorrow night,' said Alex before turning away to serve another customer.

'I'll be there.'

The smoky aroma of coffee reached Josef and drew him towards a stall with a dark blue banner that announced itself as 'Mystic Coffee'.

'What can I get you?' The woman behind the stall gave him a cheerful grin as she rubbed her hands back and forth to warm them up. The gesture reminded Josef of the chill in the air and sent a shiver though his body.

'Something hot. Just a coffee, please.'

The woman grabbed a white takeaway coffee cup and pressed down on the top of a large flask to release steaming-hot coffee into the cup. Her striking green eyes stood out against her dark curly hair. 'You just visiting?'

Josef nodded. 'A bit of a holiday, although I was born around these parts. My family moved to Germany when I was ten.'

'Ah, well, welcome home.'

Home. It hadn't been home for more than sixty years, but the town had nestled in his memories for so long that just being here felt like slipping on an old jumper and being thrilled to find that it still fitted.

'I'm Mystic. I run the coffee shop up there on Main Street.' She gestured behind and to her right. Josef followed her hand with his eyes but a stall selling knitted hats, scarves and gloves obscured the view.

'You need some gloves,' said Josef.

'I have gloves, actually. They're just not doing me any good sitting in my bag.' She passed him his coffee and offered to pour milk.

He raised his hand to stop her. 'Just black for me, thank you.'

Mystic rummaged underneath the stall, then shoved her hands into a pair of black gloves. The pale tips of her fingers and her subtle white nail polish popped out of the ends. She smiled and wiggled her fingers at him.

Josef nodded his appreciation. 'Good gloves.'

'Fingerless gloves definitely come in handy when you're standing outside for hours. You know what the weather can be like in Scotland, especially along the coast. We have our very own microclimate.'

'I remember.' Scotland had less distinct seasons than Germany. Warm, dry weather couldn't be relied upon even in the summer months, and it wasn't unusual for the typical characteristics of each season to make an appearance in the same weekend.

He had a vivid memory of building a snowman in the field beside his family home. It was autumn and he and his sisters had scraped the snow off a pile of leaves. The freezing temperature had kept the leaves crisp and the children had stuck them to the body of their snowman to form a red, brown and yellow jumper. But the following morning, the sun was splitting the sky and all that remained of their snowman was a lump of snow and a paltry pile of limp leaves, which an early-evening rain shower had then washed away completely.

Josef thanked Mystic for the coffee and weaved his way around the rest of the stalls. He thought of Alex's words as he walked. Alex had been talking about a building, of course, but his words triggered something in Josef. His bakery, like Alex's pub, was still there even though Josef wasn't. But people were different. People weren't around for long after their spouse had gone. His mother died a year after his father; Eva's mother made it eighteen months after her husband died. Barring an accident or some tragic early death, by the time people were in their seventies, the husband died first and then the wife died a short time later. That's usually what happened, wasn't it? Except it wasn't what happened in his family.

Yes, his mother had died within a year of his father, but she was ninety-three years old. His father had lived until he was one hundred. At seventy-two, Josef was at a crucial crossroads in his life. He could wither away and follow Eva sooner than either of them had planned, or he could aim to see his hundredth birthday, just as his father had done. He knew death wouldn't exactly give him a choice, but he could still aim for one outcome over the other. It was time to make a decision.

The beauty of having been married to Eva for more than fifty years was that he knew exactly what she would want him to do. Eva was still guiding him, such was the strength of her character.

9

———

JOSEF LEFT THE BED AND BREAKFAST THE FOLLOWING MORNING and stood on an empty pavement. The promenade had transformed overnight from a thriving community-centred space that filled the air with whiffs of gastronomic temptations to a barren expanse scented with nothing but the ocean. He strolled along the promenade reliving childhood memories of breezy summer days spent playing on the beach.

He and his sisters had buried their father up to his neck on this very beach more than sixty years ago. His mother had watched on, a thin scarf draped across her frame to keep the sunshine off her delicate shoulders. Her hair had been curled – he couldn't remember why – and, with her floppy hat and large sunglasses, she'd looked to Josef just like a movie star. He could see the image in his mind now as clearly as though he were looking at a photograph.

Giggles from some nearby children interrupted his thoughts and he carried on further along the promenade. He didn't know why he had never brought his own children here. He'd only brought Eva here once, before they were married. His older sister, Gisela, had returned to Scotland when she was in her thirties. She had later retired to the South of France and Josef had taken his children there many times, but never to Scotland.

Gisela was the only one of the Fischer children that hadn't been born in Scotland. She was born in Germany. Her mother had been killed in an air raid and she had lived with relatives until she was seven years old. After the war, his father had returned to Germany only briefly to collect Gisela. Josef had been born three years later and their younger sister, Adrienne, two years after that. Josef had always known that his mother was not Gisela's mother. A portrait of his father's first wife hung on their living-room wall alongside many other family photographs. It was never hidden from the children and Gisela was just as close to his mother as he and Adrienne were.

He wished now that he had planned this trip to Thistle Bay properly and had invited his sisters to join him. Gisela was in her eighties, but she had their father's genes and showed no signs of slowing down – another reason for Josef to think that he could still have many good years ahead of him.

Josef had reached the end of the promenade and could continue along the beach or head back along the streets.

'Good morning,' he heard someone say. 'Are you here for the open viewing?'

He turned in the direction of the voice and saw a gangly young man with pale skin and minimal freckles despite his orangey-red hair. 'The what?'

'To see the house.' The man flicked his hand towards the For Sale sign poking over the wall. 'There's an open viewing until noon today. I'm Chad Hernandez from the estate agents. Come in and have a look around.' Chad Hernandez. It was a distinctly un-Scottish name that didn't match his appearance at all.

Josef looked up at the house – a quaint little two-storey cottage with white walls and a sand-coloured trim around the windows. The deep-red front door was slightly ajar and positioned between two bay windows that no doubt made the most of the view across the beach and out to the Firth of Forth.

The man heaved the wrought-iron gate towards him and Josef strolled through. 'You need a bit of oil on those hinges.'

Chad laughed. 'You're right. But I can assure you there's not much else required by way of maintenance. The house is in move-in condition. May I just take your name and phone number for security reasons, please?'

Josef gave his name and watched Chad scribble it down. He didn't bother to correct the misspelling of his name and Chad didn't bother to question Josef's phone number, although Josef had caught the look of confusion on his face as he'd written down the number that was clearly not local.

Chad led Josef up the short path that cut through the middle of the well-kept lawn. Josef stepped inside the little cottage for no other reason than he had been invited to.

The short hallway was dull despite the white walls and the overhead lights being on, but there was no time for lingering as Chad was already marching on ahead of him.

'Come straight through here.' Chad made a beeline for a lounge that was likely described in the brochure as light and airy. The bay window at the front flooded the room with natural light and a wide archway through to the kitchen revealed another window to the back of the house. 'Beautiful, isn't it?'

'It is.' Josef wandered into the gloss-white kitchen. It

wasn't exactly his style, but then it didn't need to be. Tucked at the bottom of the small back garden was another building with a long narrow window running parallel to the flat roof. It was a decent size but far enough away not to shade the kitchen too much. 'What's that out the back?'

'That's the garage, although it will need a bit of work to convert it back to a garage.' Chad opened the back door and led the way to a solid wooden door, already unlocked. 'The previous occupants had a catering business that they started from home. They've moved to bigger premises now but the kitchen set-up is still here.'

Josef stepped through the doorway and into a white and stainless-steel cube. A faint odour of fresh paint lingered in the air, drawing Josef's eyes to the glistening white walls with their empty shelves just waiting to be filled. The large workspace in the centre of the room had been polished to perfection and called out for a layer of flour to be sprinkled on top.

'It's actually a double garage,' said Chad. 'It's hard to see the scale of it given the current layout but there's ample space for two cars once this lot is cleared out.'

Josef shook his head. He couldn't imagine someone tearing all of this out. Why would anyone do that? Nobody actually used their garage for their car these days anyway. 'I like it just as it is.'

Chad furrowed his brow and peered at Josef as if trying to work out whether he was a serious potential buyer or just someone killing time by checking out his neighbours' house.

The last kitchen Josef had worked in could best be described as rustic with its concrete floor, blackened stove and wooden benches. This kitchen was sleek. It was a blank canvas ready for someone new to create whatever catering business spoke to them. And the energy of this space was definitely speaking to Josef. Was it really saying what he thought it was, though?

10

Perhaps by design, The Smugglers Inn was hard to find. Josef took three wrong turns before accidentally stumbling upon the right street. The Smugglers Inn was hidden away down a dead-end street that, at first glance, looked like nothing more than a dingy alleyway. The pub itself was decidedly not dingy, however.

Only one street away from the shore, the inside was decorated like a quaint seaside watering hole. There were wooden ship's wheels on the walls, miniature sea vessels in sparkling glass bottles and lengths of old chunky fishing rope suspended from the low ceiling. Rustic barrels converted into tables were dotted throughout the inn as an alternative to the intimate booths that lined the edges of the room. The walls were painted white with blue trims – definite seaside shades with, perhaps, a nod also to the owners' Greek heritage.

Josef scanned the L-shaped pub and made his way towards the bar. Each table featured a narrow glass vase half filled with water and a lit candle bobbing on the water's surface. There were no place settings, suggesting casual dining, which very much suited him. He plonked himself down on a stool at the bar and a familiar mop of bright orangey-red hair sprung up from the other side.

'Chad.' Josef shrugged off his coat and laid it across his knees. 'What are you doing here?'

'Estate agent by day, barman by night. How are you, Mr Fischer?' To be fair to Chad, although he hadn't bothered to confirm the spelling of Josef's name earlier, he had evidently paid attention to the pronunciation of his surname with its dropped last letter.

'I'm well, thank you, Chad. How are you?'

'Feeling lucky. We're having a pub quiz and Alex and Christos always throw in a few Greek history questions.' He winked at Josef and leaned across the well-worn wooden bar towards him. 'I've been studying. I know everything there is to know about Greek gods, the Olympics, famous architecture and the population of major cities – and Christos and Alex's home towns.'

Josef couldn't help but laugh at Chad's preparation. He was a determined participant and Josef hoped it would pay off for him. 'Well, good luck to you, Chad. I'll take a beer, thanks. Something Scottish.'

'I've got just the thing.' Chad grabbed a pint glass from beneath the bar and began pouring.

'So, estate agency doesn't keep you busy enough, then?' Josef asked, intrigued by the lad's second job.

'It's a bit hit or miss. Not many properties come up for sale in this town. The owner grew up in Thistle Bay and opened her first agency here. She's grown the business and now operates across the entire east coast. I think she only keeps the Thistle Bay office open for nostalgia. It used to be busier with rentals, but more and more people are choosing short-term holiday lets instead of longer leases and they're managing those themselves.'

Chad slid Josef's beer across the bar. It had the perfect-sized creamy head and not a drop had been spilled down the glass.

'The pub business, on the other hand,' Chad continued, 'goes from busy to busier. Are you eating?'

Josef nodded. 'I promised Alex I'd check out his moussaka.'

'Excellent choice. Traditional or with a highland twist?'

'What's a highland twist?'

'Traditional moussaka with a sneaky layer of haggis. It's sensational. It's my favourite dish on the menu.'

'Well, with a recommendation like that, highland-twist moussaka it is.'

Chad disappeared towards what was presumably the kitchen, leaving Josef to sip his drink. The last pint he'd had was with Bernhard on board the Liberty. He hoped his brief drinking buddy had recovered and had been able to make it home.

Another man heaved himself onto the empty stool beside Josef and hooked his hospital-issue walking stick on the edge of the bar with practised precision. 'Are we ready to win this thing, boys?' Josef caught a whiff of tobacco as he spoke. 'You're new. I'm Charlie.'

'Josef.'

'Welcome to the winning team, Joey. You'll be glad you chose to sit up here. That's Jimmy, and he's Lenny.'

Jimmy leaned forwards on his seat and reached across Charlie to shake Josef's hand. 'Good to meet you, Josef. I'm James, actually.'

Charlie shrugged his shoulders. 'James. Jimmy. It's the same thing.' He passed sheets of paper that had been torn from a spiral notebook to the men clustered around the bar while Lenny, who introduced himself to Josef as Lennox, handed out tiny pencils like the kind golfers use for marking up their scorecards.

Despite his advancing years, Lennox had a thick head of dark hair with only a sprinkling of silver around his ears. He sat on the other side of Josef. With a trim physique and straight spine, he looked like a golfer. Josef pushed his shoulders back and sat a little straighter.

The others were a bit older, in their seventies like him, he guessed, and probably creaked a little more than they would have liked. Maybe he should take up golf, he thought.

Chad delivered refreshments to the trio without being asked – a whisky, two pints of lager and three packets of peanuts. Charlie scooped up the whisky and Chad slid an extra bag of peanuts Josef's way.

Josef smiled as Mystic squeezed herself in between him and Lennox. She ordered a glass of red wine and a gin and tonic. 'Hi, it's good to see you again,' she said.

Charlie cleared his throat dramatically. 'Don't be trying to poach our new team member, Mystic. Joey here is on our team and I'm feeling good about our chances tonight.'

Josef had half expected Charlie to call her Misty, although he suspected Mystic was the kind of person who wouldn't hesitate to put Charlie in his place if she needed to.

'Drinks are on you gents later, then.' Mystic scooped up the drinks that Chad had laid on the bar for her, then Josef watched her strut away.

He turned back to the bar just as Alex arrived from the kitchen with a plate of food. 'Are you ready for a feast, my friend?' He gripped the edges of the plate with a spotless white tea towel and placed the meal in front of Josef.

The moussaka was a perfect square of deliciousness

with a golden top that still sizzled with the heat. Alex handed him a fork and gestured for him to tuck in. Josef dug into a corner of the moussaka and scooped up enough food to include each of the layers. Alex grinned as he watched Josef eat, seemingly confident that his dish would be well received. The combination of rich tomato and lamb with the creamy béchamel sauce and the aubergines created a spectacular flavour. The haggis gave the dish a sumptuous extra something without detracting from the authenticity of the dish.

'Just as good as any moussaka I've eaten in Greece itself, young man,' said Josef, to Alex's obvious delight.

'I'm so glad you like it. It's my mother's recipe with a nod to our beautiful surroundings here.'

Josef dived in for another mouthful, giving Alex a broad smile as the man returned to his kitchen.

As he ate, Josef listened to Charlie giving the rundown on who he thought was their biggest competition for the quiz. He had savagely dismissed all but two groups as not having what it takes to beat them.

'Mystic might be our main competition,' said Charlie. 'The woman knows a little bit about everything and that's key for a quiz champion. But we've got numbers on her tonight, boys.' He slapped Josef on the back. 'With Joey here, we've got an extra team member.'

'Are we allowed that?' asked Josef. 'Shouldn't the teams have the same number of members?'

'We don't worry about things like that here,' said Charlie.

'It only matters if you lose to a big team,' added James. 'Then we complain, of course.'

Charlie shook his head. 'All's fair in love, war and pub quizzes.' He drained his glass and gestured towards Chad, who appeared in seconds with a bottle of Johnnie Walker. He poured the amber-coloured liquid into Charlie's glass without the aid of a measure. 'You ready to lose again tonight, lad?' Charlie asked Chad.

Josef caught a hint of uncertainty in Chad's eyes before he smiled and shook his head. 'I've got the edge tonight, I think.'

Charlie slapped Josef on the back again. 'You're not as well travelled as our boy here though, are you?'

Chad's smile faltered and he nodded to the far end of the room. 'We'll soon find out.'

'Here we go, boys.' Charlie rubbed his hands together and snatched his pencil from the bar.

Christos stood at the back of the room on a narrow stage raised about two feet off the ground. He had a bulging belly not unlike Josef's own, his dark hair was cropped close to his head and his facial hair was neatly trimmed. He tapped on a microphone and the din in the bar ceased. The pub patrons turned their attention to him as he waved a pale blue folder in the air.

'Before we get to question one, can I please reiterate the pub quiz rules?'

Josef heard Charlie scoff behind him.

'Firstly, let's remember that the quiz is a bit of fun. The winners must not gloat or demonstrate bad sportsmanship.' His gruff tone seemed an unnecessary mood killer.

'Secondly,' he went on, 'anyone smashing glasses or throwing crockery or cutlery will forfeit their right to play in next week's quiz.'

'What on earth?' Josef mumbled and caught Chad flicking his eyes towards Charlie. Oh boy. Josef suddenly wondered if he was on the right team.

'Let's begin.' Christos slipped a sheet of paper out of his

folder and Josef spun around on his bar stool to join his teammates. 'Question one. Which Fife city was once the capital of Scotland?'

'Dunfermline,' Charlie whispered confidently.

'Question two. In ancient Greece, what was the prize for the winners in the Olympic Games?'

James circled his head with his hand and earned a smack on the arm from Charlie. Josef scribbled 'crown of olive leaves' on his paper.

'Question three. Whisky cannot be called Scotch whisky until it has been aged in Scotland for how many years?'

Josef shrugged. Whisky wasn't his tipple of choice. Charlie anchored his hand close to his chest and held up three fingers.

'Question four. Which philosopher was the teacher of Alexander the Great?'

Chad had his brow furrowed and tapped his pen erratically on his notepad. It looked as though philosophy wasn't one of the subjects the boy had studied.

'Aristotle,' whispered Lennox.

'Question five. Mary Queen of Scots was imprisoned on Castle Island in which loch?'

'Too easy,' murmured Charlie.

Josef smiled and wrote 'Loch Leven' on his paper. His father had taken him trout fishing on that loch when he was just a boy and he remembered seeing the castle from their boat.

'Question six. Architect Norman Foster led the reconstruction of which famous German landmark?'

Charlie looked blankly at his teammates. Josef wrote 'Reichstag' on his paper and turned it to the group. Charlie copied it down with childlike enthusiasm and guffawed out loud. 'Our secret weapon,' he said, gripping Josef on the shoulder. 'We've got this, boys.'

Josef felt the crowd turn their eyes towards his group and he feared he was about to witness the reason for Christos's pub quiz rules. He put his head down and concentrated on the sheet of paper in front of him, filling in the answers he knew and leaving a space for those he didn't.

By the time Christos had finished the questions and had run through the answers, Charlie was practically bouncing in his seat. They had won by a single point. Charlie had been right. Mystic's team had finished in second place.

'Congratulations, gentlemen,' said Christos. He tucked the microphone behind the bar and came towards them holding out a blue marker pen. He leaned towards Charlie. 'Be nice.'

Charlie snatched the pen then grabbed his walking stick. He chortled out loud as he hobbled his way to a board on the wall a few feet away. 'We're back in the lead, boys,' he yelled as he wrote their names on the board in handwriting twice the height of everyone else's. 'Watch and learn, kids. The oldies will show you how it's done.'

James and Lennox shook their heads and spun their bodies back to the bar to distance themselves from Charlie's show.

'Life experience,' Charlie bellowed once he had finished writing up their names. 'That's the difference. Forget about your fancy education. It doesn't matter if you don't let yourself experience life. Isn't that right, young Chad?'

Christos plucked the microphone from behind the bar. 'Remember the rules, people. Let's be gracious winners.'

Everyone in the bar must have known Christos's words were aimed at Charlie but the majority of patrons had turned their attention to Chad, who had busied himself rearranging bottles of whisky on a shelf behind the bar. The poor boy's neck was a fiery shade of red. Josef glanced at James and Lennox, who rolled their eyes and took a glug of their pints.

'Me and the boys will see you all next week.' Charlie thrust his metal walking stick in the direction of the other teams. 'That's if anyone bothers to show up. There's no point, really, is there? We'll only show you up again.'

Charlie hee-hawed his way back to the bar and plonked himself down beside Josef, his raucous celebration at an end.

'That was quite the win, Charlie. What are you like when you lose?' Josef asked.

'Hasn't happened yet, Joey.'

James cleared his throat and Charlie sighed.

'Maybe once or twice,' said Charlie.

The rest of the evening was filled with good conversation and lots of laughter. Even Charlie was surprisingly good-natured once the competition was out of his system and he had downed another whisky. He regaled the group with stories of his days working as a distiller and he still, he said, gave tours around the distillery during the peak tourist season.

'I hope you're friendlier to the tourists than you are to your quiz competitors,' said Josef.

James and Lennox snickered and raised their glasses to Josef.

'It's called passion, boys,' said Charlie, although even he was unable to keep a straight face.

Josef emptied his glass in one last gulp and lumbered off his seat. 'Time for me to head back.'

Lennox stood up too. 'I'll walk with you. You staying at Gloria's?'

'The bed and breakfast? Yes.'

Chad dashed along the bar towards them and scooped up Josef's empty glass. 'Goodnight, Mr Fischer,' he said.

Josef sensed his speed had less to do with wanting to clear the empty glasses and was instead related to his estate-agency day job, although Chad was discreet enough not to mention the viewing.

'Out with it, laddie,' said Charlie and Chad's pale skin turned red for the second time that evening.

'What?' said Chad.

'You're never normally so eager to see us off the premises. What's going on?'

Chad shook his head. 'Nothing's going on.'

Josef chuckled and decided to throw Chad a rope to pull himself out of the hole he'd inadvertently fallen into. 'I was looking at a house today. Chad's just reminding me to call him about it.'

'What house?' asked James.

'A cottage along the other end of the promenade,' said Josef.

'The Patels' old place,' said Charlie with a nod. 'Lovely house.'

James slid his empty glass towards Chad and hopped off his bar stool. 'As you might imagine, Charlie here has an opinion about out-of-towners buying property in Thistle Bay.'

Charlie shook his head. 'I don't care where you're from as long as you want to live here. What I can't abide are out-of-towners buying property for holiday lets. We have some beautiful houses in this town that sit empty for nine months of the year. That's not right. And it prices young folk, like our Chad, out of the market.'

'If I buy anything, it'll be for me,' said Josef. 'But I probably won't be buying. I only came for a holiday.'

Chad's shoulders slumped and Josef felt as though he had ruined the boy's night.

'We've heard that story before,' said Lennox with a grin.

'Aye,' added Charlie. 'Jimmy came for a holiday and never left.'

James nodded. 'It's a hard town to leave.'

Josef shoved his arms into his coat and pulled it up around his neck. 'My children want me to move to Stuttgart and live with my son.'

Charlie unhooked his walking stick from the bar and rose to his feet. 'That's kids for you. They forget we've been making decisions for ourselves since before they were alive. We don't need them to parent us. We have lunch here every Friday. If you're still here, come and join us.'

'And if you're around next Tuesday, there's a yoga class at the studio on Emerald Street,' said James.

Josef tilted his head. He couldn't quite see his drinking buddy on his hands and knees in Lycra.

Charlie scoffed. 'Hippy nonsense.'

James scowled. 'It's a powerful exercise. People who do yoga live longer.'

Lennox clasped his hands together and practised swinging an imaginary golf club with obvious competence. 'You'd all be better off hitting a few balls on the course with me. I'm healthier looking than the lot of you.' He turned to Josef. 'No offence.'

Josef laughed and patted his stomach as it strained through his olive green gingham shirt. 'None taken.'

James stalked off ahead of them. 'One of these days I'm going to get you all to a class. I'll have the fire brigade on standby ready to hoist you off your mat when you're done.'

They said goodnight to Chad, left the pub and dispersed in different directions. Josef shoved his hands into his coat pockets and sauntered back towards the bed and breakfast alone.

He glanced up at the cosy glow in the windows of his accommodation and strolled on by. Three minutes later he stood in front of the squeaky iron gate of the cottage for sale. He rested his hands on the cold metal, closed his eyes and pictured Eva's face.

Plenty of people thrived when they lived alongside their children. But not Eva. She would never have moved in with any of hers. That would have seemed like accepting she was entering the final phase of her life. That's what his children thought about him, and he couldn't blame them. Losing their mother in her seventies must have made the mortality of their father seem all too close. Whatever time Josef had left, he knew for sure that Eva would want him to truly live it.

Was he crazy? Was he blinded by grief? Or was he thinking clearer than he had in weeks? He didn't know. All he knew was that when he thought about buying the little cottage on the promenade, with the ocean view and ready-made bakery in the back garden, he felt a tingle in his gut that had served him well throughout his life.

11

———

'You did what?' bellowed Nadja into the phone.

Josef sighed. The conversation with his daughter was unfolding just as he had predicted. She'd had a fiery nature since the day she was born and, when she wasn't trying to make the decisions herself, she was used to at least being consulted on any decisions that affected her parents.

'I know it's a big change, darling, but come and look at the house and you'll see how much sense it makes.' Josef sliced his sultana scone in half whilst his daughter collected her thoughts and made multiple huffing noises. He plucked the gold-foil-wrapped butter portion from the side of his plate and warmed it between the palms of his hands, a gesture he'd seen Eva do many times.

'You're not thinking straight, Dad. You should be close to family at this point in your life, not a thousand kilometres away.' Nadja sounded almost desperate.

'Are you OK, Nadja? Has something happened?'

'Yes, something has happened. My mother died suddenly and now my father has taken himself off to a different country and has just called me to say he's not coming back.'

Josef glanced around Mystic Coffee. The fire crackling nearby and the scent of freshly ground coffee beans told him he was in the right place. He could, of course, find a charming coffee shop with a fire in Germany – he'd been in plenty over the years – but his arrival in Thistle Bay had felt like coming home. Sitting here now, with softened butter in his hands and his daughter grumping at him over the phone, he savoured the lightness in his body that he hadn't felt since Eva had died.

'I know this seems sudden, Nadja, but your mother and I always intended to do a bit of travelling in our retirement. You know that. We didn't want to stay still before we had to.'

Nadja sighed into the receiver and Josef could picture her lips narrowing and transforming into a poker-straight line as they always did when she was trying to keep her anger in check.

'Dad, you and Mum had plans to split your time between your children and grandchildren. You didn't plan on moving to Scotland. None of your children live there.'

'I still plan to split my time between you all. It's just that I hope to have a lot of life left and I have to build something for me in that life.'

The bell chimed above the coffee-shop door and Josef swung round instinctively. A group of older women bustled in, chatting and laughing about something. They reminded him of Eva and her friends on their weekly visits to his bakery for free coffee and cakes. Despite Eva only having visited Thistle Bay that once, everywhere he looked reminded him of his wife. Whether he stayed in Berlin, decamped to either of his sons' homes, or remained here in Thistle Bay, Eva would be with him. He was sure of that.

Josef spotted Chad hurrying across the street towards the coffee shop and he told Nadja he'd call her back later. Chad bustled in the door with his blue folder clutched against his chest and a massive grin on his face.

'Hello, Mr Fischer,' he said as he reached Josef's table.

'Hello, Mr Hernandez. Can I get you something to drink?'

Chad shook his head. 'No, thank you.' He opened his folder and pulled out a stack of papers. 'Are we really doing this?'

Josef nodded. 'We are.'

Josef's phone buzzed on the table beside him and he knew without looking that it was Nadja messaging him. He unlocked the phone and read the text.

Sign nothing. I'm on the first flight tomorrow.

Josef smiled as he pictured his daughter frantically booking a last-minute plane ticket. He didn't want to worry his children, but he didn't want to be beholden to them, or, worse, be a burden. If he lived as long as his father, Josef had another twenty-eight years of life left. And he wanted to live it.

He looked up at Chad, who was perched, papers poised, on the end of the chair. Nadja was going to be furious with him, but his gut once again told him he was doing the right thing. 'Do you have a pen?'

12

JOSEF SAT WAITING FOR HIS DAUGHTER IN THE BRIGHT GUEST lounge at the front of the bed and breakfast. Despite the chill outside, the sun streamed through the glass and warmed the room. A red Volkswagen Polo pulled up outside and Josef sprang up to help Nadja unload her suitcase. She had refused his offer to meet her at the airport.

Before he was even out of the lounge, the bell above the front door chimed and Nadja flew in, wheeling a small black suitcase behind her.

Josef expected to see fury on her face. Instead, he saw an ashen complexion and her forehead lined with worry. Eva had been the parent who offered hugs and soothing words; Josef's usual response was to feed someone who was in pain by baking something sweet. This time, he had nothing edible to offer. He held out his arms and Nadja fell into them, holding him tighter than she had ever held him before.

Josef rubbed his hand back and forth across his daughter's back. 'I'm sorry, Nadja. This is just something I have to do.'

She pulled back to look at him. 'I know you think that, Dad, but now isn't the time to be making big decisions.'

'Your mother and I had already made the decision. We were selling the house and moving to the coast.'

'Yes. The German coast.'

'The North Sea.' Josef pointed out of the window. 'And that's the North Sea out there.'

Nadja raised her eyebrows and glared at him.

'It's not the same, I know that,' Josef conceded. 'But nothing is the same.'

Nadja cleared her throat and rubbed at her face.

Josef grabbed the handle of her suitcase and tilted it onto its wheels. 'Let's get you checked in and we'll go and get something to eat. There's plenty of time to talk about this.'

Mystic's coffee shop was buzzing with lunchtime energy when they arrived. Above the muffled conversations, a baby whined with impatient hunger, an oven beeped somewhere behind the counter, and the bell above the door chimed every minute as people left and others joined the queue behind them.

'What are you hungry for?' Josef asked.

'Just a coffee,' Nadja said.

When it was their turn to be served, Mystic gave them a broad smile and said hello to Nadja. 'You must be Josef's daughter. I'm Mystic.'

'I'm Nadja. Pleased to meet you.'

'What can I get you?' Mystic asked.

'I'll take a vanilla latte, please.' Josef shook his head at her order. He could never understand why Nadja was a fan of coffees that came with frothy milk and syrups that did nothing except blunt the flavour of the coffee. 'And a black coffee for my dad.'

'And something sweet,' added Josef. 'Whatever you have.'

Mystic smiled. 'I've got just the thing. Let me clear a table for you in the window. The town looks very pretty when the sun is shining.'

Josef and Nadja followed Mystic to a table at the front of the coffee shop. Mystic scooped up the empty mugs and a plate and popped them on the counter behind her. Susie, Mystic's barista, passed her a spray bottle. She spritzed the table, wiped it clean with a cloth and guided Nadja to the seat facing down Main Street and towards the sea. Josef dropped into the seat opposite her.

They sat in silence until Mystic returned with their coffees and two slices of carrot cake. 'Here you go,' said Mystic. She handed Nadja a fork. 'This should put some colour back in your cheeks.'

Josef accepted the other fork and thanked Mystic as she walked away.

Nadja took a long gulp of coffee and a forkful of carrot cake. Josef followed her lead and tucked into his cake, appreciating that whoever had baked it had been heavy-handed with the pecans.

Mystic had been right. Colour reappeared on Nadja's face as she ate and Josef thought it wise to keep quiet until she was ready to talk. There was no point in making small talk when the one thing they needed to talk about was huge. At least, Nadja felt like it was huge. It didn't feel that way to Josef, but he understood why it might do to his children.

Nadja speared the last piece of her cake and chewed slowly. She wiped her lips with her napkin and took another sip of coffee. 'Dad, you must understand how this looks to us.'

'I do, darling. Of course I do. But two of you already live

in other countries. Is it really so inconceivable that I might want to do that too?'

'But you're . . .'

'Old?'

'That wasn't what I was going to say.'

'You were thinking it, though.'

Nadja smiled. 'Maybe.'

'There are two paths in front of me, Nadja. I can follow your mother *now* or *later*. I'm choosing later. It's what I would have wanted for your mother and I'm sure it's what she would want for me.'

He knew his daughter couldn't argue with that one. It was the same argument he had used to justify going on the cruise on his own and it had the same effect this time. It silenced Nadja because she knew he was right. Her eyes flitted between him and the view from the window as she formulated what else she wanted to say.

He spoke again. 'It's not so crazy. I'm from here. I lived here for ten years.'

'Yes, but that was sixty years ago, Dad. It's the wrong decision.'

Josef nodded. 'Perhaps. But it's not an irreversible one.'

It had been a long time since he had thought about Thistle Bay, but he'd been here only five days and felt as though he had slotted back in to somewhere comfortable and comforting. In those few days, he had laughed, he had made friends, and he had glimpsed a different future to the one he had seen while sitting in his living room in Berlin. It was a different future to the one he still wished he could have had. But it was a future that gave him a morsel of excitement, and he knew he had to cling to that.

Josef was pulled from his thoughts by a tap on the window. A grinning Chad stood on the street outside with a set of keys dangling from his hand. He dashed inside the coffee shop and appeared next to Josef.

Chad dropped the keys onto the table in front of Josef. 'I was just on my way to see you.' Then he said hello to Nadja, oblivious to the tension in the atmosphere.

'Chad, this is my daughter. Nadja, this is Chad Hernandez.'

Nadja said a polite hello and Chad shook her hand.

'It's so great to meet you,' said Chad. 'It's lucky you're here today. Those are the keys to your dad's new place and I imagine you're itching to have a look around.'

Nadja folded her arms across her body and Josef jumped in with a 'Thank you, Chad' before his irritated daughter could get a chance to say anything.

'I don't need to come with you,' added Chad. 'Just drop the keys by the office once you're done.'

Chad disappeared as quickly as he'd arrived and Josef smiled at the trusting nature of people in small towns. He picked up the keys. He didn't expect his daughter to fall in love with the house and the new life it promised the way he had done. But he hoped it might at least make her feel a little better about what he was planning to do.

'Shall we go and have a look?' he asked.

Nadja put her head in her hands and groaned. 'I suppose we ought to.'

13

Nine weeks later, Josef dusted icing sugar over his tray of Berliners as Nadja watched from the doorway. The garage kitchen at the Thistle Bay cottage was everything he'd imagined it would be. The sparkling-clean surfaces were ample enough to hold his mixing machine, baking trays and cooling racks with plenty of workspace left over. The industrial-sized fridge and ovens were more than sufficient for his needs. He'd purposely kept his street kiosk small so his daily bakes could fill the front of the stall without requiring an overwhelming amount of work on his part.

Despite his children encouraging him to stay retired, kneading dough and glazing pastry relaxed him, and selling his bounty and interacting with customers brought him joy. He no longer had a reason to give up these small pleasures.

'Are you almost ready to go, Dad?'

Nadja had softened in the week that she'd spent with him in Thistle Bay. He couldn't describe her as being happy with his decision to stay, but she had given up trying to talk him out of it and had instead focused her attention on making sure he had everything he needed to launch his new venture. Not that he needed much – he already had the bakery and he had ordered his wooden stall online and had it constructed on the agreed site on the Friday before he had returned to Thistle Bay.

His street-trader's licence came through surprisingly quickly, helped no doubt by the minuscule and towable nature of his stall. He had thought his preferred location on the promenade might be objectionable but the helpful lady he'd dealt with in the local council office had described his venture as 'essentially an ice-cream truck selling cakes'. He hadn't known what she meant until he'd seen the ice-cream van appear on the promenade one Saturday morning. Josef's stall looked nothing like a truck, but if an ice-cream truck could park up in a prime location all day, there was no reason his stall couldn't occupy space in that same location. Both the bakery and the stall had passed their environmental-health inspections the day before and he was officially ready to sell his baked goods to the public. Now here he was, ready to trade.

Josef stood back and admired the two trays of Berliners he had just dusted. He planned to offer only one or two types of product each day, alternating between a dozen or so different options. Custard-filled Berliners had been Eva's favourite and they seemed a fitting recipe for launch day.

'Let me cover these and I'm ready to go,' said Josef.

Nadja helped him load the trays into the tiny blue car he had bought for transporting his bakes from his garage to the stall on the promenade. The journey took all of five minutes to drive down and unload the cakes and another few minutes to take the car home again.

Once they'd walked back along the promenade from his house, Josef stood and admired his stall. The red wooden frame was even more polished and professional than he had imagined. He had space for two display trays plus a small counter to handle cash and card payments. The heat lamp above the display space was switched off, but he'd trialled it and it warmed up quickly – perfect for pastries that were best served warm. His two trays bursting with Berliners completed the look.

'Ten minutes each morning and my business is up and running.'

'You still need a name,' said Nadja.

'I'm waiting for inspiration.'

Josef's children had all helped him come up with a list of words, both English and German, that people would associate with a bakery. Nothing had felt right. He wasn't in a hurry, though. He liked the informal nature of it all and he knew a name would come to him eventually.

His plan was to catch the breakfast trade on weekdays, possibly open a little later and longer on weekends, plus the occasional evening depending on what was going on in the town. He had the luxury of working when he wanted to and not because he needed the money to support his family.

'Good morning.'

Josef started at the voice that came from behind and turned to see Mystic wrapped in an ankle-skimming coat and brimming with cheer as she crossed the road towards him.

'You look too happy for this time of the morning,' grumbled Nadja.

'When your business serves breakfast, you have to make the effort.' Mystic's eyes scanned the trays of Berliners.

'You're my first customer so a Berliner for your breakfast is free of charge.' Josef selected a perfectly round cake with his tongs and slid it into a paper bag.

Mystic smiled and held out one of the takeaway coffee cups in her hands. 'I'll swap you. A Berliner for a coffee.'

'Deal,' said Josef. He wrapped his hands around the paper coffee cup and a swash of steam escaped through the lid carrying the welcome aroma of strong coffee. He handed Mystic her cake and she raised the bag towards him in thanks.

'I brought a vanilla latte in case you were here too.' She handed the other coffee to Nadja, who snatched it up with glee.

'That's really kind of you,' said Nadja. She took a swig and closed her eyes. 'Just what I needed. It's so early. I've been trying to persuade Dad not to open the stall at such an ungodly hour.'

Josef laughed. 'And I've been telling her, when you get to my age, you're up at this time of the morning anyway.'

Mystic nodded her agreement, although Josef guessed she was at least twenty years younger than him.

'As much as I love my bed,' said Mystic, 'a sunrise in Thistle Bay is worth getting up for.'

Nadja gazed out towards the sea and Josef caught the changing light on her face. Her pale skin was warmed by the orange sky. He knew that expecting her to be happy with his decision was still too much to ask at this point, but her smile told Josef she would leave Thistle Bay content that her ageing father was just fine.

Mystic plucked something from her coat pocket and handed Josef a small package wrapped in brown paper with a deep-purple ribbon. 'Here's a little something to keep you cosy between customers.'

Josef tugged until the ribbon gave way and hooked his finger under the fold at the end of the package. He chuckled as he pulled out a pair of black knitted gloves. Fingerless, of course.

'They're perfect, Mystic. How very thoughtful of you. Thank you.'

Mystic smiled. 'You're welcome. Now, I've got bacon to cook. Good to see you again, Nadja, and safe travels in case I don't see you again before you head home.'

'Thank you. And thank you for the coffee.'

Mystic marched back up Main Street and disappeared into her coffee shop just a few doors up.

'I can't say I'm happy about leaving you here, Dad, but it seems as though you have a good set-up. Mum would have liked it here.'

Josef ambled out from behind his stall and wrapped his arm around his daughter's shoulders. 'I think so too.'

AUTHOR'S NOTE TO THE READER

A letter from Claire

Dear Reader,

Thank you so much for reading *New Beginnings*. You can catch up with Josef again in *Sunrise in Thistle Bay*. As I was writing *Sunrise in Thistle Bay*, I knew I wanted to further explore Josef's background and what led him to Thistle Bay.

I felt Josef's pain so deeply when I was writing his story and I just had to send him Lilli, the undertaker, to help him through it. Her arrival brought a tear to my eye.

One of my favourite scenes in the book is The Smugglers Inn pub quiz. Josef's teammates are a quirky bunch. I think we all know a Charlie! Lennox, the golfer, reappears in book 3 - Snowfall and Second Chances. I hope you'll enjoy finding out more about him.

If you enjoyed *New Beginnings*, please consider leaving a rating or review. Hearing from readers and receiving reviews is both amazing and a little frightening, but reviews help other readers to take a chance on new authors and I would love for more people to discover Josef.

Thank you again for reading.

Claire x

ABOUT THE AUTHOR

Claire Anders was born and raised in a seaside town in Scotland. She now lives in Edinburgh with her husband and daughter. When she's not writing, you can usually find her walking her dog in the nearby woods or with a book in one hand and chocolate in the other.

Between Moons was Claire's first historical fiction novel. Claire also writes contemporary feel-good fiction with a touch of romance. All of her books feature strong friendships and supportive communities with a secret or two thrown into the mix.

 facebook.com/claireandersauthor

ALSO BY CLAIRE ANDERS

Historical Fiction

Between Moons - A gripping WWII historical novel

~

Contemporary Fiction

Sunrise in Thistle Bay - An uplifting small-tcwn romance

New Beginnings - A Thistle Bay Short Story

Snowfall and Second Chances - A festive feel-good romance

SUNRISE IN THISTLE BAY

Sometimes the only way forward is to go back.

A childhood in care has left Cat Radcliffe craving connection and a place to call home. When she takes an assignment for a company in the Scottish seaside town of Thistle Bay, her focus is on doing the work well to get a good reference for her fledgling copywriting business.

Nick Bell has lived in Thistle Bay his entire life. His last girlfriend headed to London to escape small-town living and he vowed not to get involved with another city girl. When he meets Cat, he knows he should ignore his growing attraction for the girl who's lived in eight cities in as many years.

Just as Cat is beginning to make plans for the future, an explosive secret shatters her world and sends her running back to the city.

Sunrise in Thistle Bay is a story of family, forgiveness and self-discovery.

Fall in love with Thistle Bay.

SNOWFALL AND SECOND CHANCES

Is it ever too late for a second chance?

Jeremy Lewis left Thistle Bay two decades ago to join the Marines. But five years ago, his one-night stand with childhood sweetheart Rebecca resulted in their twin boys. Now Jeremy is leaving the Marines and is determined to reclaim his family – including Rebecca.

Rebecca Knight is used to doing everything for everyone. She puts herself second, always. Being a single mother and working in her family's business full-time has been tough for her. With Jeremy moving back to town, Rebecca had thought it was finally time for their second chance. But with big changes at work, she doesn't have the time needed to make a relationship work.

While Jeremy focuses on building his new business, Rebecca finds herself torn between her career and love.

Can a relationship that's been neglected for so long still have a chance?

Snowfall and Second Chances is part of the Thistle Bay series. It can be read as a standalone novel, but it contains a spoiler if you haven't read *Sunrise in Thistle Bay*.

SUNRISE IN THISTLE BAY
SAMPLE CHAPTERS

CHAPTER 1

Cat pushed her trolley of suitcases through the open doors of Edinburgh Airport's arrivals hall and scanned the white cards held by people dressed in an array of wildly different styles. Her eyes fixed on her own name, Catherine Radcliffe. She had expected it to say Thistle Bay Chocolate Company. On the handful of occasions she had been collected at an airport for work purposes, the card had always had the company name written on it.

The man holding the card was one of the more smartly dressed individuals. He wore a black suit, white shirt and a dark green tie. He wouldn't have been out of place at a funeral.

'Hi,' said Cat, managing to sound brighter than she felt. 'That's me.'

'Miss Radcliffe. Welcome to Scotland.' The man stepped beside her and took over the handlebar of her trolley. 'Allow me. I'm Arthur.' He placed the name card on top of her cases and steered the trolley through the horde of people gathered by the doors. 'How was your flight?'

'It was good, thanks.' Cat played along with the usual

airport small talk as they exited the terminal and walked to the car – black, of course – which was parked in a bay on the ground floor of the multi-storey car park. Arthur stowed her suitcases in the large boot and opened the rear passenger door of the sleek Mercedes.

'I'll return your trolley,' he said. 'You get yourself settled.'

Cat stared into the back of the car. This was the last part of her journey. The immaculate leather seats and the freshly vacuumed carpet in the footwells should have been inviting after fifteen hours of travelling. Instead, the hair on the nape of her neck lifted and beads of sweat dampened her collar.

'Everything OK, Miss Radcliffe?' asked Arthur, arriving back at the car.

'Actually, would you mind if I sat in the front?'

Arthur closed the rear door and opened the front passenger one instead. 'If that's what you would prefer. You get travel sick, do you?'

'Something like that.'

People who knew her story always presumed Cat would want to sit in the back of a car. After all, it was being in the back that had likely saved her life in the head-on collision that had claimed the lives of her beloved adoptive parents when she was six. But she preferred to sit in the front. The higher chance of death didn't bother her. *You're dead – you don't know about it*, she had always thought. *The problem is what you miss when you can't see in front of you.*

It had happened two years after the accident. Cat still remembered the crunching of tyres on the gravel driveway, the car pulling up in front of a house as she looked out of the window to see where they were stopping. Hartsfield Children's Centre. She could still feel the chill that had spread through her eight-year-old body, the look on her foster mother's face that told Cat everything she needed to know as she'd opened the car door for her to get out of the back seat. Cat had said nothing as she was led inside the building, her foster father trailing behind with her rucksack and a cardboard box. They'd all sat in a room with orange fabric chairs and a chipped coffee table while a woman introduced herself only as Mo. And then came those words that had stung her so badly as a child: 'With our own baby on the way,' her foster mother had said with a hand on her swollen stomach, 'we don't think we can help you become the person you are capable of becoming. We thought it best to let it happen as quickly as possible for you.' Those words that, as an adult, she saw were just a cop out – the kind of thing that people said when trying to make themselves feel better for doing things they knew weren't right. There had been no discussion, no time to prepare.

But Cat couldn't be angry. Biology mattered. It's why the adoptive parents who had loved her so much had always made sure she knew she had another mother somewhere despite Cat being too young back then to really understand. It's why her best friend Rachel still took care of her own birth mother despite twenty years of drug addiction that had left Rachel to be raised in care alongside Cat. And it's why Cat continued to search for biological relatives despite so many years of goose chases and dead-ends. There were no official records. If her adoptive parents had known any details, the drunk driver who'd hit their car when Cat was still so young had made sure they weren't around to tell her. Cat had been alone in the world since then.

Cat sat in the front seat of Arthur's car, the cool leather a welcome sensation to counteract the heat that had risen in her while staring at the back seat.

'One of my boys used to get travel sick,' said Arthur, putting on his seatbelt. 'He was always better in the front.

You'll find some water in the side of the door there and you just let me know if you need fresh air or for me to pull over, Miss Radcliffe.'

Cat opened the bottle of water and took a sip. 'I'll be fine from here, honestly. And please call me Cat.'

'OK then, Cat. Let's get you to Thistle Bay.' Arthur fired up the engine and pulled away.

'Thanks, Arthur. Let's hope the traffic is light at this time of night so you can drop me off and get back here at a reasonable time.'

'I'm from Thistle Bay actually. When I get you there, I'm already home.'

Cat glanced over at Arthur in his smart suit and swanky car. 'I wouldn't have thought there'd be much call in Thistle Bay for a professional driver.'

'You'd be right about that. I work for Mr Knight and the family – driving, deliveries, and anything else they need me to do, which includes picking up VIPs like yourself from the airport, although I'm usually taking them to the Edinburgh facility. It's not often I drive them all the way to Thistle Bay.'

Cat had never been described as a VIP before and she suddenly worried that Alan Knight, the CEO of Thistle Bay Chocolate Company, had greater expectations than she did about what she could deliver for his business.

The Forth Road Bridge loomed up on their right but instead of veering towards it, the car kept going.

'Oh, I haven't been on the new bridge before,' said Cat.

'Aye. The Queensferry Crossing. The three bridges over the water is quite a sight.'

The new bridge hadn't existed when Cat had last lived in Edinburgh, and as a visitor in the years since, she hadn't strayed too far from the city centre. Given how many years it takes to construct a bridge, perhaps the passage of time had changed more than just the view across the Firth of Forth.

'I thought you'd be American, you know. But are you a local lass?'

'I moved to Edinburgh when I was eight and lived here until I left university at twenty-two.'

'You didn't pick up much of an American twang while you were there.'

Cat had always had an accent that people found hard to place. The thick London accent she'd spoken with since she was old enough to talk had quickly faded when she'd ended up back in foster care, in Edinburgh. But she hadn't taken on a completely Scottish accent. To the Scots she sounded English; to the English she sounded Scottish.

'I was only in the US for a year – although it's easy to find yourself copying the accent a bit when you're surrounded by it all day.'

'And are you heading back there after your time with us?'

'I haven't decided yet,' said Cat. She was planning to go and stay with Rachel for a while after this assignment was finished and, right now, her best friend's spare room in Edinburgh city centre was about as far in the future as she could see.

When she'd lost her job, she'd also lost her visa. Launching a copywriting business had been part of a failed attempt to transfer visa categories. But she'd attracted clients and hadn't been as fazed by the uncertainty of it as she had expected to be. Self-employment gave her the freedom to go wherever she wanted to go; she just had to maintain a steady stream of clients to keep her income up.

Heading to Thistle Bay didn't thrill her – it was too close to a past she'd tried to shut off – but the assignment itself could be fantastic. Alan Knight had offered her two weeks' work rewriting his company's entire website. It was a significant project, and having a multimillion-pound corporation on her portfolio would add credibility to both her and her embryonic business. All she had to do was make sure she had happy clients at the end of the job.

The takeaway coffee cup in Arthur's cup holder was emblazoned with the words Mystic Coffee in dark blue block lettering.

'I've never heard of Mystic Coffee,' said Cat. 'Are they an Edinburgh chain?'

'No. Mystic's is in Thistle Bay, but her coffee could rival any from those fancy Edinburgh places and is much better than the stuff at the big coffee chains.'

'That's good to know. I need a good strong coffee to wake me up in the mornings.'

It wasn't long before the Mercedes had left the busy dual carriageway and was heading along deserted country roads bordered by fields and the occasional farmhouse that cast a shadow on the darkening sky.

There was a road sign just before the roundabout that indicated 'Thistle Bay 1 mile'. Cat took a deep breath. She couldn't wait to get into her room at the bed and breakfast Alan Knight had booked for her. She needed a shower and to go through the notes she'd made before her first meeting with the company. Thanks to the business-class lounge access that Alan had arranged for her, she'd already eaten dinner, which saved her from having to hunt for somewhere to find food. But the first thing she wanted to do was stretch her legs and get some fresh air to ease her pounding head.

'Is it your first time in Thistle Bay?' Arthur asked.

'Yes.' Despite all of those years she'd lived in Edinburgh, she had never visited any of the Fife seaside towns. The car climbed a gentle hill and Cat leaned forward to get a better view of the town once they reached the top.

Their arrival in Thistle Bay was pretty underwhelming. Cat had expected to see the town stretched out in front of her with lights glowing in the windows of tiny cottages. Instead, she saw nothing but a row of plain-looking houses. One thing was clear – there weren't any buildings higher than two storeys.

Arthur manoeuvred the car along narrow roads and Cat smiled as, street by street, the town began to reveal its charm. The further into the centre Arthur drove, the more the scenery shifted to match the image she'd had in her mind. Pavements widened as residential areas gave way to the town's hub. Independent businesses lined the main road with their pastel-painted shopfronts. Hanging baskets of autumnal flowers still bursting with colour hung at intervals from the Victorian-style lampposts dotted along the kerbside. It was the kind of location she could imagine a film crew pitching up at to shoot a cosy murder-mystery drama series with a middle-aged amateur sleuth solving grizzly crimes in between bake sales and summer fêtes.

The car crawled along a street that led down towards the sea. 'Here we are,' said Arthur.

'Wow, that sunset is something else,' said Cat. The orange glow of the sun sinking into the sea created a trail all the way across the water that was broken only by the silhouette of a single wind turbine.

'Aye, we do a lovely chocolate and a sunset like no other here in Thistle Bay.'

Arthur turned the car at the end of the street and stopped in front of the first building. The exterior of the bed and breakfast looked exactly as Cat had expected. The double-storey building was painted white with black trims and had the cosy glow in each of the windows that she had hoped the entire town would have had. From the outside, at least, it looked just as cute as the photos on the website.

The cool evening air hit Cat when she opened the car door, along with an intoxicating scent of sweet cinnamon and caramelised sugar that brought back memories of Edinburgh's Christmas markets. It was coming from a small market stall opposite the bed and breakfast – the only stall along the entire length of the promenade. It had no obvious signage but its red frame and warm light from a heat lamp above two metal trays called out to Cat.

'Arthur, oh my gosh. Is that guy selling real sugared almonds?'

'Smells like it,' said Arthur, sniffing the air.

'I need some. Can you give me a minute?'

'Sure. I'll unload your luggage.'

Cat crossed the empty road and the man mixing the almonds caught her eye. He was older – in his seventies at least, Cat estimated – with a good head of grey hair peeking out from beneath a white cap. He wore a short-sleeved white T-shirt with a burgundy-red apron that stretched over his bulging stomach.

'I see you're tempted by my almonds,' he said in a thick German accent as Cat approached.

'I am,' she said. 'I love real sugared almonds, but I haven't had them in so long.'

'Try one.' He held out a stainless-steel scoop with an almond balanced on the end.

Cat took the almond and crunched it in her mouth. It was still warm and tasted like Christmas with its sweet yet spicy flavour. Cat hadn't had a family Christmas since she was little girl but she still loved everything about the season, especially the food and drinks.

'Delicious. I'll take two bags, please.'

'You have good taste,' the man said. 'Have you just arrived?' He filled a pink-and-white-striped paper bag with almonds and nipped it closed at the top. Passing it to Cat, he moved on to the second bag.

'Yes. I'm doing some work here so I'll be in town for a couple of weeks.'

'Excellent. I'm Josef. You stop by here anytime.'

'I will. I'm Cat, and thank you for these – such an unexpected treat.' She handed Josef cash and headed back towards the bed and breakfast.

Arthur was waiting on the wide pavement beside his car as Cat returned with her bulging paper cones. She popped one in her handbag and passed the other to Arthur.

'Thank you for the ride, Arthur. This one is for you.' She rummaged in her handbag with her free hand. 'Now, let me get you a proper tip.'

'Oh, no, there's really no need. I can't accept that. But I won't say no to these.' He took the almonds, unfolded the top of the bag and peeked inside. 'Your luggage is in the lobby, and I'll see you in the morning. About eight thirty?'

'Perfect,' said Cat. She waved Arthur off and moved to go inside and check in.

The entrance to Thistle Bay Bed and Breakfast sat directly on the pavement, although it was evident someone had tried to establish a garden feel. Planters in front of each window bulged with bright purple and pale pink flowers that looked like giant daisies, there was a wooden bench pushed up against the building's façade and bright blue pots of shrubs were placed in a row to create a short path to the front door.

Cat didn't expect anyone minded the obstacles since the pavement was plenty wide enough.

Cat pushed open the door and a bell chimed above her head. She smiled at the quaint metal bell that rocked back and forth before she spotted a woman with glistening silver hair waiting beside her suitcases.

'Hi, you must be Mrs Murphy,' said Cat.

'Call me Gloria. Goodness, look at you.'

Cat tucked her shoulder-length brown hair behind her ears. She'd had her layers trimmed just before leaving Los Angeles but she could imagine her hair was now plastered to her head after the journey. She smoothed her hands down her crumpled dress. There wasn't a crease on Gloria's blue jumper and, noticing the woman's chunky fuchsia necklace and freshly applied pink lipstick, Cat felt dishevelled. 'I've just come off a long flight.'

'Oh, no – sorry, hen. You look lovely. It's just you look like someone I've met before.'

'Really? Well, it's my first time here so it can't have been me.'

Gloria shook her head. 'No, it wasn't.' Her voice seemed to crack slightly and she cleared her throat. 'Let's get you checked in. Catherine Radcliffe, right?'

'Yes, and you can call me Cat.'

'You're the last guest to check in tonight. Let me get your key and I'll show you around.'

After taking Gloria's lead and poking her head into the immaculate eight-table dining room and the snug guest lounge, Cat made her way up the narrow staircase. Following the directions Gloria had given her, she found her door and put her key in the lock. She couldn't remember the last time she'd stayed in a hotel that had an actual key rather than a key card. She pushed the door open and fumbled for a light switch.

Inside was a generous-sized room and a bay window with a view of the sea. It was more homely, and bigger, than some of the flats Cat had lived in. Paying back her student loans hadn't left much of her salary for rent during her first few jobs. She'd wanted to be tied to those loans for as short a period as possible so had always paid back more than the minimum instalment due and had cleared them completely within four years of graduating.

Cat wheeled two of her suitcases into the room and Gloria appeared behind her with the final one, her already rosy cheeks now a little rosier from the exertion of hauling the suitcase up the stairs.

'Probably not what you're used to, hen. I expect Los Angeles is much fancier than my wee B&B.'

Cat took in the crisp white bedding with a lilac throw and two cushions, each adorned with a thistle print, propped against the fluffy pillows. The cream carpet was springy beneath her feet and the walls were a combination of light wood panelling on the lower half and ivory wallpaper with an embossed floral pattern on the upper half.

'It's lovely,' said Cat. 'And the view is amazing – I can't wait to see it properly in the morning.'

'I'm glad you like it. The rooms are all similar, but I keep this window for guests of Mr Knight, if I can.'

Cat was going to ask how Gloria knew Alan, but in a town with 1,400 people – as her research had told her – of course she would know him.

Instead, it was Gloria who asked, 'Have you known Mr Knight long?'

Cat shook her head. 'I've only met him once, actually.

But that's why I'm here. To get to know the family and the business a bit more.'

Gloria stood staring, lips pursed, as if waiting for further explanation.

'I'm a copywriter, so I'm rewriting their website for them.' On paper, Alan was taking a risk giving such a big project to her new company, but during their meeting in Los Angeles he had seemed quite taken by her thorough research, and perhaps knowing that she'd grown up across the water from his business had given him an extra slice of reassurance. That proximity was the main reason Cat had been reluctant to take the job, but she'd been left with no choice and, now that she was here, she was completely focused on the job and determined to impress him.

'I'd better let you settle and get some sleep,' said Gloria, closing the door and leaving Cat alone.

Cat's eyes dropped to the luggage that literally contained everything she owned. Renting furnished flats meant Cat had never acquired much stuff, and she didn't have a child-hood bedroom or space in her parents' attic to store away memories. The only thing she had from her childhood was a photo album of the first six years of her life with Jessie and Joe, her adoptive parents. Cat had been taken into care with nothing but the clothes she was wearing at the time of the accident. She later presumed it was her mother's brother who had tied up her parents' estate after they died. The only thing that had made it back to her was the photo album – it was the one symbol of home she owned and it was the thing she turned to whenever she had a big decision to make.

Cat unzipped the shoulder bag she'd taken with her on the flight, tugged the album free and laid it on the rustic oak bedside table. It fell open at a photograph of Cat dressed as Sophie from Roald Dahl's *The BFG*. Cat had watched the

BFG movie over and over again as a small child. Her mother, Jessie, had worried that the scary giants might give her nightmares but Cat had never dwelt on them. For Halloween, Jessie had made her a yellow dress with huge stitches joining the seams and bought her an orange wig and round-framed glasses. Cat had insisted her father, Joe, pretend to be the Big Friendly Giant. But then the worst had happened. Jessie and Joe, the only real parents she could remember having, had been taken from her overnight and, like Sophie, Cat had ended up in a children's home. Only Cat knew no one would come for her. This was the reason she looked at the album so sparingly. Each photograph invoked fond memories, but the bitter ones crept in too.

She still remembered her first day in a courtroom. Her parents' funeral hadn't even taken place and here she was, six years old, sitting behind a shiny wooden desk that she could only just see over while lawyers and social workers decided her fate. 'And the child has no other relatives to take her in?' the Judge had boomed from his platform at the front of the room. He'd reminded Cat of the BFG with his big ears and bushy white eyebrows – only he wasn't friendly. He didn't speak to her. He didn't even glance in her direction. 'No relatives that are *able* to take her in,' had come the reply from a flame-haired woman who'd introduced herself to Cat only moments before the hearing. That first court appearance was over in minutes. Cat had said nothing. No one had asked her to speak. She'd felt as though no one even knew she was there.

Cat moved to five different foster homes before relocating from London to Edinburgh. When she found herself back in a children's care facility, she realised no one was ever going to ask for her views. To be heard, she would have to step up and use her voice, whether invited to or not. So she did. It didn't change her childhood, but she grew into a self-assured woman who was skilled in her job and undaunted by relocating to new cities – new countries, even – on her own.

Cat closed her photo album, her palm lingering for a few seconds on the bronze leather cover, before picking up her phone. She logged in to her Find My Family account to check her messages. It had been fifty-two days since she'd read the words that made her skin tingle with nervous anticipation: 'You have a DNA match.' She had reached out immediately to the blank avatar identified only as CocoB13 – the only person who might be able to tell Cat who she was and where she came from.

She had played out so many scenarios in her mind. CocoB13 was her mother who had spent thirty years regretting the decision to give her baby away on the night she was born. Or her father who hadn't known of her existence until she had swabbed her DNA and made it available online for anyone that paid the registration fee to compare their own DNA against. Or perhaps it was a half-sister or half-brother. Of course, it would probably turn out to be some cousin twice removed who knew nothing about her mum – but even that would be further than she'd ever managed to get on her own.

She knew most people just did DNA profiling for fun, but finding out she was seventy-six per cent European gave her nothing new. She needed her DNA match to make contact with her if she was ever going to learn more. If they'd bothered to go through all the hassle of registering their details, surely they would follow it up.

Cat refreshed her screen. Inbox empty. She had to ration the number of times a day she accessed the app – the disappointment was taking its toll and it was proving to be nothing but a distraction. She opened her phone's settings and turned on her email alerts. Find My Family would email her when she had a reply. She usually kept notifications turned off for email so they didn't interrupt her flow when she was working, but turning them on felt like the only way to stop torturing herself with the app.

She turned back to the view from the bay window. The sun was gone completely now but the dusky blue sky was just light enough for her to still see the beach. Her head was fuzzy from the flight. Or perhaps it was from a swell of emotion that had been building inside her since her stop-off in London. Either way, a walk on the beach could only help. And she wanted to find the chocolate shop so she knew where she was going in the morning.

Cat pulled on her coat, snatched the sugared almonds from inside her bag and left the bed and breakfast without running into Gloria or any other guests. The only sign of life outdoors was the glow from Josef's heat lamps lighting up his frame as he mixed a tray of almonds, probably hoping for a few more sales before he headed home.

Seconds later, Cat was on the beach. Slipping off her tan-brown shoes, she sunk her feet into the sand and took a deep breath. She hadn't been looking forward to coming back to Scotland but, now she was here, she'd make the best of it and focus on doing a good job. She'd figure out where to go next once the job was finished. She unzipped her coat. The early-evening temperature was milder than she expected and Cat inhaled a deep breath. There really was no air like Scottish air.

CHAPTER 2

The cool sand between Cat's toes felt magical and, with the gentle lapping of the waves on the shoreline, was already helping to clear the fuzzy head that came with half a day of travelling. She popped an almond in her mouth and crunched, breaking through the gnarly, sugary coating.

Walking down to the water, she had to negotiate a wide strip of egg-sized stones and dried seaweed that separated the dry sand from the wet. She had slipped her shoes off too early. Cat braced herself, stepped onto the stones and scuttled over them as quickly as she could. The address for the chocolate shop was Main Street, the same as Gloria's address, so it had to be further along the promenade, she reasoned. She'd make her way there by following the shoreline as it ran parallel with the street.

She sauntered along the beach for a few minutes when a dog appeared out of the darkness in front of her and dropped a miniature orange rugby ball on a rope at Cat's feet.

'Oh, hi,' said Cat, crouching down to pet the dog. 'Where did you come from?'

The jet-black dog wagged its tail fervently. Cat ran her hand through the dog's damp hair and it nuzzled into her knee. She scanned the beach for an owner but it was too dark by now to see properly.

'Skye. Here, girl!' sounded a voice from further along the beach.

'Are you Skye?' Cat said, and the dog turned in a circle and pounced on its ball with its front paws.

'Skye,' came the voice again, a bit closer now.

'She's over here,' yelled Cat. She scratched the dog behind the ears, sand from its fur pressing beneath her fingernails. 'Are you in trouble?'

'I'm sorry. Is she bothering you? Skye, here!'

The light from the moon up above illuminated Skye's owner as it bounced off the royal-blue sports shorts and T-shirt he wore. Sweat had turned his thick, blond hair dark at the edges of his face, suggesting he'd been out for a run along the beach when Skye had abandoned him and sought Cat's company instead. He had a deep suntan, discernible even by moonlight, which hinted at a lot of time spent outdoors, and his blue eyes reflected the shimmer from the sea.

Skye picked up her ball and bounded over to him. He bent down, prised the ball from her mouth and threw it back along the beach. The dog gave chase and disappeared into the blackness.

'It's really dark along there. Aren't you worried you'll lose her again?' said Cat, straightening up.

The dog came thundering back seconds later and dropped the ball at Cat's feet again.

'She always finds me,' he said.

The panting dog gazed up at Cat, tongue hanging out and tail wagging.

'She wants you to throw her ball, but don't worry, I'll get it. I'm Nick, by the way. And you've met Skye.'

'I'm Cat.' Cat bent down to pick up Skye's ball.

'I wouldn't,' said Nick. 'It's soggy from slobbers and the sea.'

Cat picked the ball up by the rope. She could handle a slobbery ball. She whipped her arm back and round and released the rope. The ball shot off to her left towards the promenade pavement and Skye ran away into the darkness ahead of her.

'Oops,' said Cat, hoping the lack of light would hide the flush on her cheeks.

'I bet you couldn't do that again if you tried. I'll get it.'

Nick jogged off and found the ball in seconds. He squeaked it as he walked back to her and Skye came tearing back towards the sound. Nick threw the ball down into the sea. No doubt exactly where he had intended it to go.

'Are you just visiting?' he asked.

'Is it that obvious?'

'Yeah, but only because it's a tiny town and I know I've not seen you around before.'

'I'm doing some work for Thistle Bay Chocolate Company. I arrived about an hour ago so I was taking a quick walk to find out where the shop is for tomorrow.'

'Well, you're going in completely the wrong direction. A bit like that ball.'

Cat looked down at her hands and pretended to brush sand off them. Great. She couldn't throw a ball or navigate her way around this tiny town. 'I was taking the scenic route,' she said. 'I needed to stretch my legs after the flight.'

'Given it's dark, you'd be better taking the direct route,' said Nick, pointing behind her. 'Where have you arrived from?'

'Los Angeles.'

Nick whistled and the dog scampered towards them. 'That's a long way to come just to visit a chocolate shop.'

'I'm a copywriter. I'm doing some work on their website so I'll be here for two weeks.'

Skye seemed to have had enough of chasing her ball around and criss-crossed in front of them, the dripping rope hanging from her mouth, as they headed back along the beach.

Cat padded over the wet sand, the occasional icy wave covering her toes. Nick, a good six inches taller than Cat, walked alongside her.

'The beach is so peaceful . . .' She let out a loud yelp as something jagged caught the side of her foot, causing a searing pain, and she fell into Nick as she hopped about and grabbed her foot.

Nick gripped her arms to steady her. 'What was that?'

'I don't know,' she shrieked, rubbing her stinging foot. 'Something bit me.'

'OK, just breathe,' said Nick, still holding her up. 'I don't see anything on the sand.'

'It must have come from the water.'

'Probably a jellyfish.'

Cat gasped. 'Are they poisonous?'

'Not the ones round here,' he said. 'You need to rinse your foot in the sea.'

'I'm not sticking my foot in there,' said Cat, taking a painful step back. 'And before you say it, I'm not going to pee on myself either.'

Nick laughed. 'That's definitely not what I was going to say. But you *are* going to have to put your foot in the sea.'

Cat shook her head. 'What if it's still in there?'

Nick took his hands away from her arms just by an inch

to make sure she was stable. He bent over, untied the laces on his trainers and prised them off his feet. He then tugged his socks off and tucked them inside one of his shoes.

'What are you doing?' Cat asked.

'Showing you there's nothing to be scared of.' He stepped into the sea and swirled the water around with his foot. 'See, nothing there. Now, come over here.'

Cat reached for Nick's outstretched hand and limped into the water. She gave a sharp intake of breath. It was freezing cold. She wanted to jump back out again but Nick probably already thought she was a baby without her needing to prove it further.

Nick, still holding her hand, used his foot to flush water around hers. He bent down a little to see what he was doing and they came face to face, his warm breath on her skin. His grip on her hand was tight and comforting and it was easy to ignore the sting in her foot with so many other sensations stirring in her body.

'That should do it,' said Nick. 'Let's get you off the beach. Skye, come!'

Skye, having ignored the commotion and continued further along the beach, now sprinted back to Nick.

'Can you walk on your foot?'

She said she could and they both stepped out of the water and back onto the sand.

'You sure?' He waited for her nod before he released her hand.

Nick collected his trainers and they made their way off the sand and back onto the promenade path. He put his sandy feet directly into his shoes and stuffed his socks in his pocket.

Cat held the wall to steady herself as she brushed sand off her feet, one at a time, as best she could and put her shoes back on. Skye, looking for attention, nuzzled her wet nose against Cat's bare leg.

'Is she a springer spaniel? She's quite small.'

'A working cocker spaniel.'

'I see you.' Cat scratched the spaniel on the top of her head for a few seconds. 'You're a needy one, aren't you?'

'She's not needy, she's loving.' Nick sank down near the ground and called Skye over to him. The dog hid her head behind Cat's leg and didn't budge.

'She doesn't seem to be loving you right now.'

Nick shook his head at the dog. 'She's loving, but fickle. Come on, have a seat over there.'

Cat followed Nick to a bench on the promenade and sat down. He gestured for her to lift her foot.

'It's fine now, really,' she said.

'I just want to check there's no sting in it.'

Cat slipped her shoe off, held her floral-print dress on her knee and lifted her foot. Nick cupped her ankle and held on to her toes with his other hand. He twisted her foot around to pick up light from the nearby lamppost.

'I don't see anything. It's just a little swollen and red. Soak your foot in hot water tonight and you'll be fine.'

'Thank you, Doctor Nick.' She had meant it sincerely but the words somehow came out with a sarcastic edge. 'Really,' she added.

'Are you staying at Gloria's?' asked Nick.

'I take it you don't have many bed and breakfasts in town.'

'Just the one. I'll walk you over there.'

'No, honestly, it's fine. Besides, I still want to find the chocolate shop before I go back.'

'You should really soak that foot.'

'I will. It won't take me long to find the shop.'

Nick glanced around him. 'It's on my way so I'll walk you there.' He picked up Cat's shoe and put it back on her foot, then clipped Skye's lead on and pocketed her ball. 'When you come out of Gloria's, turn right and you're on Main Street. The chocolate shop is at the very top of the street.'

They meandered along the promenade and Cat couldn't help but think how romantic a walk this would be under different circumstances. The sea was calm, the waves giving only the occasional gurgle, and patches of light shone on the dark street under the ornate lampposts. If she ignored the throbbing on the side of her foot, the cool air was a welcome change from a scorching Los Angeles summer.

They reached Josef's stall and he appeared to be packing up for the night. The scent of hot sugared almonds still lingered in the air and Cat took a deep breath and smiled as she caught Josef's eye.

'Goodnight, Cat,' the old man said. 'I hope you enjoyed your almonds.'

Cat patted the paper bag tucked inside her coat pocket. 'They were wonderful, thank you, Josef.'

Josef beamed and nodded his head. He waved to Nick as they turned to cross the street before he disappeared beneath the counter to continue closing up his stall.

'You like your food, then,' said Nick, tugging on Skye's lead to keep her moving when she tried to stop and sniff the postbox.

'Excuse me?'

'You've been here an hour and you're already on first-name terms at the local food stall.'

Cat glanced at Nick, unsure if he was making a joke or having a dig at her. His neutral expression didn't help her decide which one it was.

They walked straight up Main Street and there it was –

the Thistle Bay Chocolate Company shop. The streetlights gave off enough light for her to see the signage. She peered in the windows but all she saw were shadows; she would have to wait until the morning to get a proper look. First impressions were good, though. The location was great. It wasn't right on the beachfront but in daylight it must have a view of the beach, and the sign looked big enough to be seen from the promenade.

'Is the factory nearby?' asked Cat.

Nick pointed to the left-hand side of the shop. 'It's behind that wall, there.'

But it was too dark to see anything more. She'd wanted to see where the shop was and she'd done that now, so time to go back and soak her foot – although the throbbing had dulled already.

'Do you think you'll remember the way tomorrow?' It was Nick's turn to sound sarcastic, only Cat was sure his tone was actually intended.

Cat smirked. 'I think so. I also remember the way back to Gloria's, so thank you.'

'Skye and I will make sure you get back to Gloria's safely. We're heading that way.'

'Don't you live up here somewhere? You said the shop was on your way.'

'Actually, we live on the promenade. Your internal compass seemed a tad out of order and I didn't want to spend the night worrying about whether or not you made it to the shop.'

Cat put her hand on her hip. 'There was no need. I would have found it on my own. And even if I had gone off in the wrong direction, doesn't it take, like, ten minutes to walk around the entire town?'

Nick laughed. 'Not quite, but you make a good point.'

They strolled back towards Gloria's and another sign caught Cat's eye with its familiar deep-blue block lettering. 'There's Mystic Coffee,' she said. 'I'll be stopping off there tomorrow morning.'

The coffee shop was in darkness too. She'd forgotten that things closed earlier in small towns. She was used to stepping outside and picking up a takeaway coffee at any time of day or night. Coffee was a lifesaver when she had a deadline looming and needed something to keep her awake until she had finished her project.

'It's the best coffee in town,' said Nick.

Skye stopped to sniff a lamppost. She seemed intent on inspecting them all. Cat didn't mind. The fresh air had lifted her headache and, despite her earlier embarrassment, she wasn't in a rush to end her walk with Nick. She was quite content listening to him giving her the rundown of Mystic Coffee's food menu. Apparently it was where most of Gloria's guests ate lunch and the occasional early dinner.

'If you want to eat later, there's the local pub, The Smugglers Inn. The owners are from Greece and the food is authentic Greek cuisine. They also do takeaway,' said Nick. 'Other than that, you'd need to get a taxi out of town. There's not a lot choice around here but the food is homemade and delicious.'

Main Street was annoyingly short and two minutes later they were already standing in front of Gloria's. Cat scuffed her shoes against the edge of the kerb, reluctant to turn her feet in the direction of the bed and breakfast. She bent down to give Skye one last pat. 'Goodnight, cutie,' she said. The little spaniel closed her black eyes and stood perfectly still, revelling in the attention.

When Cat stood up, Nick was smiling at her. For a second she imagined she was in Los Angeles and free to give in to her overwhelming desire to reach out and kiss him. You're working, she reminded herself. And he thinks you're a hapless idiot.

'There you are, hen,' said Gloria. 'I was just locking up. Evening, Nick.'

'Evening, Gloria.' His voice was cheery, no sign of disappointment that their moment had been interrupted.

'If you ever need another sat-nav,' he said to Cat, 'just let me know.' He put his hand on her shoulder as he stepped off the kerb and a heat spread through her body. She wanted to turn and watch him walk away, wanted to see if he glanced back at her like in the movies, but Gloria was looking at her, waiting for her to go in.

'Soak that foot,' Nick said from behind her, giving her the opportunity to turn. He was standing in the middle of the road, his eyes locked on her. She smiled and nodded, then forced herself to turn away and go into the bed and breakfast.

Cat climbed the stairs to her room, curled up on the bed and powered up her laptop. She had to forget about Nick. She may have made a fool of herself on day one in Thistle Bay, but tomorrow was the day that mattered. Just seeing the chocolate shop had sparked some ideas and she was keen to note them down. Her foot would have to wait. This was only the fifth client of her fledgling freelance career but her biggest one to date and if the commission went well she could use it to attract more business.

The chime of a video call coming through interrupted her furious typing and Rachel's number flashed on the screen. Cat clicked Answer to accept the call.

Rachel Barnes, Cat's best friend, waved into the camera from the living room of her tenement flat in Edinburgh.

'Urgh! I was hoping your LA glow would have faded on the flight. You make me embarrassed with my pasty skin.'

'Nonsense, you're gorgeous,' said Cat. 'Your pale skin helps the bright blue of your eyes to sparkle.'

Rachel's eyes were a piercing blue that stood out against her porcelain complexion and chocolate-brown hair. Cat had experimented with hair dye over the years to brighten up her hair. She had the classic shade of mousy brown that made her look washed out when she wasn't sporting a Los Angeles suntan. Whereas Cat had no idea if her hair colour came from her mother or her father, Rachel knew her colouring came from her dad. Although she couldn't remember him, she'd shown Cat a few pictures that her mum, Heather, had kept. Besides, Cat knew Heather had blonde hair and naturally golden skin, although her complexion had transformed into a grey pallor as a result of long-term substance abuse.

'I might still break out the fake tan before we meet for mojitos.' Rachel clasped her hands in a prayer position under her chin. 'Friday, isn't it?'

'Nice try.'

'Oh, come on. I can't wait a fortnight to see you.'

When Cat had arrived at Hartsfield Children's Centre in Edinburgh she was already considered too old to be adopted. Rachel was already there, having fallen into a pattern of rotating in and out of Hartsfield each time Heather cleaned herself up then relapsed again. The longest block of time Rachel ever spent with her mother was five months, which was also the longest she and Cat went without speaking to each other. On the day Rachel arrived back at Hartsfield after that absence, her cheeks stained with tears and disappointment, she'd said that she hadn't visited Cat for fear it would tempt fate and push Heather to once again choose drugs over her daughter. For years after that, Rachel lived in hope that Heather would one day sort herself out so they could become the proper family Rachel had always longed for. Cat, on the other hand, accepted that she wouldn't leave Hartsfield until she was old enough to live on her own.

Now her friend was only an hour away and Cat was dodging seeing her.

'This town is seriously tiny,' Cat said. 'I don't want the Knights to think they're paying me to socialise. I just need to get the work done and then I'll be free to have as many cocktails as you want.'

'I don't think they'll mind you having one drink with your oldest friend.'

'Probably not. But I just want the job to go perfectly.'

'Are you sure you're not just avoiding dealing with the fact that you're home?'

'I'm not home.'

'Look,' said Rachel. 'I know you have this need to travel the world and find yourself or whatever, but the location doesn't actually matter. You've been to eight cities in eight years and what's changed? Maybe it's time to stop searching for a place that feels like home and just set up a home for yourself.'

Cat sighed at the familiar speech. Rachel had been asking Cat to come home for at least the last three years. But Cat had never considered Edinburgh her home. It was just the city she had grown up in, and the place she left as soon as she could. Cat touched the dark mobile phone on the bed beside her to light up her screensaver. It was a picture of her and Rachel on a rare sunny day at the Edinburgh International Book Festival in Charlotte Square Gardens. As a copywriter and a high-school English teacher, Cat and

Rachel found that the book festival provided the perfect platform for an annual get-together. Edinburgh was a great place to be a tourist, but Cat didn't want to live there again.

Her first move had been to London because that was where she'd lived with her parents after being given up for adoption by her birth mother. She'd been so certain she would settle there, build a life and put down some roots. She found a job and a room for rent in a shared house but instead of the homecoming she'd expected, it was a reminder of everything she had lost – the opportunity to know her birth mother; the chance to be part of a family. Five months later and Cat was on the move again. She had been avoiding London and moving every year or two ever since.

Now, here she was. Thirty years old and about to end up right back where she started – homeless in Edinburgh.

Not wanting to succumb to her despair, Cat changed the subject. 'I just met a guy on the beach.'

Rachel squealed with delight as she probed for details. Thinking about Nick for another half an hour couldn't hurt.

I hope you enjoyed this sample of *Sunrise in Thistle Bay*.

Download the ebook or order the paperback to continue Cat's journey.

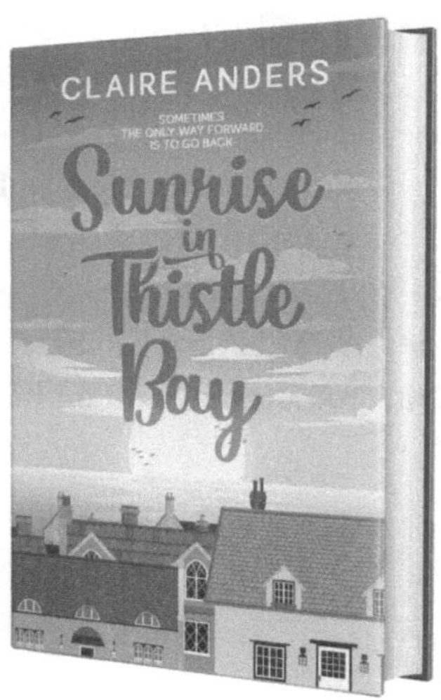